CHAOS BEGINS

EMP Collapse Book One

CHRISTINE KERSEY

The characters and events portrayed in this book are fictitious. Any similarity to real persons, living or dead, is coincidental and not intended by the author.

Chaos Begins (EMP Collapse Book One)

Copyright © 2021 by Christine Kersey

All rights reserved

Cover by Novak Illustration

No part of this book may be reproduced, or stored in a retrieval system, or transmitted in any form or by any means, electronic, mechanical, photocopying, recording, or otherwise, without express written permission of the publisher.

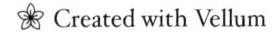

❦ Created with Vellum

NOTE FROM THE AUTHOR

This is a work of fiction. Although this story takes place in and around Salt Lake City, Utah, the areas described may not be exactly like the real locations and are only intended to lend a sense of authenticity.

CHAPTER 1

Melissa

WHEN THE POWER WENT OUT, Melissa Clark's first thought was that she hadn't saved the changes to her PowerPoint presentation before her computer had abruptly shut off. The presentation was due at the end of the day and it was already two-thirty. How was she going to get it done now? Groaning in frustration, she realized how dark it was. With her cubicle in the basement of the building in downtown Salt Lake City and no window in her cube, the darkness was nearly absolute.

Like a moth drawn to a porch light, when Melissa noticed sunshine trickling in through a high but small window in her co-worker's cubicle across the way, she pushed back from her desk and headed directly there. "Hey," she said to Tamara before sitting in an empty chair beside her friend's desk.

Tamara was frantically writing something on a notepad in the dim light. "Hang on a sec." After a few moments she set the pen down and turned to Melissa. "Sorry. I was in the middle of writing a great email response when the power went out." She grinned. "I didn't want to forget my brilliant reply."

Melissa chuckled, until she remembered her PowerPoint. "Yeah, I lost some of my brilliant work."

Tamara grimaced in reply, then she smiled. "Maybe we can go home early."

"I wouldn't mind that, except I have to finish that presentation." She softly sighed. "Guess I can do it from home. I'm sure the power's on there."

"Yeah."

Craning her head to see a strip of blue sky out of the high basement window in Tamara's cubicle, Melissa smiled. "In the meantime, maybe we can enjoy the rest of this beautiful day. I mean, even though it's March, it's not too cold out."

Tamara nodded. "True. It's at least forty degrees."

Another co-worker, Rob, stepped into the space. "Hey, let's go into the hallway. There should be emergency lights on out there."

The women agreed and followed Rob through the dark office space toward the door that led to the hallway. He opened the door, which was when they saw that the hallway was just as dark as their office.

"That's weird," Rob said. "The emergency lights should be on."

"Maybe they don't come on right away," Tamara suggested.

Melissa reached into her pocket and pulled out her cell.

"Let me turn on my flashlight app." She pressed the button to wake her phone, but nothing happened. "Huh."

"What's wrong?" Tamara asked.

Continuing to press the button, Melissa frowned. "My phone won't turn on."

In the darkness, she could barely make out Tamara and Rob trying their phones.

"Mine's not working either," Rob said.

"What the heck?" Tamara said. "Mine's dead too."

Melissa turned back the way they'd come and squinted in the direction of the main part of the office where there was a bit of light coming in through a pair of small, high windows. Though she couldn't see a whole lot, she could see there were people there and she could hear them talking. "Let's see what everyone else is doing."

The three of them began to make their way toward the voices, careful not to run in to anything in the weak light. After a few moments they joined the larger group who stood near the windows. Light seeped into the space, but it was less than adequate. One of the men was tapping at his cell phone. "Hey, Colin," he said to another man in the group, "is your cell phone working? Mine won't turn on."

Colin pressed a few buttons. "Nope. Mine's dead too."

"So are ours," Melissa said to the group as a sense of foreboding washed over her.

"That's really odd," Colin said. "I mean, even if all the cell towers were disabled somehow, that wouldn't kill the phones completely."

"What about some sort of power surge?" asked someone else.

"What kind of power surge would be strong enough to take out cell phones that aren't even plugged into a wall outlet?" Colin asked.

The more she mulled it over, the more Melissa thought she knew what might have occurred. As a fan of post-apocalyptic fiction, she'd read about this kind of thing, although she'd never imagined it would actually happen. Shoving aside images of all the horrible things that might be on the horizon, she softly exhaled before speaking. "An EMP would do it." Her voice was soft, but all eyes swiveled in her direction.

"An EMP?" a man in a suit asked, his voice filled with incredulity.

Wondering how many of her co-workers knew what an EMP was, she said, "An Electromagnetic Pulse could take out the power grid and our cell phones."

"Holy crap," someone muttered.

"What would cause an EMP?" a woman asked.

"I can think of two things," she said. "One, a nuclear explosion detonating miles above us in the atmosphere. Or two, a really big solar flare called a Coronal Mass Ejection."

"A solar flare wouldn't cause this," a man said, disbelief thick in his voice.

"Actually, it already has," Rob said. "Ever heard of the Carrington Event?"

Melissa was grateful to have someone else back up her

claim. Not that it really mattered. Something terrible had happened whether people wanted to believe it or not.

"No," the man said in reply to Rob. "What's that?"

"Back in 1859 there was a CME," he nodded toward Melissa, "a Coronal Mass Ejection. It's called the Carrington Event. It wreaked havoc on the telegraph system, in some cases sending sparks through the lines and setting paper on fire."

"That doesn't sound like that big of a deal," the man said.

Rob chuckled. "Not if your biggest technology is a telegraph system. But nowadays, with everything computerized, imagine everything being hit by something that powerful." He did a chin lift toward the space where they stood and all the desks with computer monitors on them. "Now it would be a big deal. A very big deal. Like, catastrophic."

"So, you think it was a CME?" someone asked.

He nodded toward Melissa again. "Or a nuclear explosion high in the atmosphere like Melissa said. That would take out all the electronics."

"I think it's time to go home," Tamara said.

"If our cars work," Rob said.

Oh crap. Melissa had forgotten that an EMP would kill most of the cars.

"Our cars?" Tamara asked.

"Yeah," Rob said. "Unless it's a really old car. Like, pre-1970's old. Anything newer has electronic components. An EMP would take those out which means those cars won't work."

"Are you sure?" Tamara asked with hope lighting her voice.

Desperately hoping that she and Rob were wrong, Melissa said, "Only one way to find out."

The group began moving toward a nearby stairwell that would take them up to the ground floor. Following them, Melissa didn't bother to stop and get her car keys from her purse stashed in her cubicle. The usefulness of her nearly new car would be obvious soon enough when her coworkers tried to start theirs.

Feeling her way up the stairs, she eventually reached the first floor along with everyone else. With large glass doors at both ends of the hallway, plenty of light filled the space. A few people were standing around talking in small groups.

"Where are you guys going?" one man called to Melissa's group.

"To see if our cars will start," Rob answered.

"Why *wouldn't* they start?" the man asked, his eyebrows tugging together in obvious confusion.

"We think there's been an EMP," Rob answered.

Everyone who had been standing around in the hallway was listening to the exchange.

"Are you kidding?" someone asked.

Rob shook his head, then moved toward the door that led to the parking lot. Melissa and everyone else followed. Those who had their car keys went to their cars. Melissa watched as they climbed in.

Tamara stopped next to Melissa. "Do you really think they won't start?" she asked.

Still hoping she was wrong, when Melissa saw someone get out of a car wearing an expression of both fear and disbelief, she knew she was right. Heart clenching with the realization that this was the beginning of something unimaginable, Melissa bit her lip and glanced at Tamara but didn't reply.

One by one, each person who had tried to start their car stepped out of their vehicle wearing the same shell-shocked look.

"This is crazy," Tamara murmured.

Shoving down her concerns, Melissa turned to Tamara with a grimace. "Now I wish I'd worn more comfortable shoes."

"Why do you say that?" Tamara asked.

"Unless you have a bicycle stashed somewhere around here, you and the rest of us will be walking home."

"Oh my gosh," Tamara said. "That's, like, fifteen miles."

Melissa glanced at her own three-inch-heel boots that she wore with her slacks. They were comfortable enough to wear at work but walking home in them would be a challenge. "I know. I live twenty miles from here." As she thought about the time it would take to walk that distance, she knew there was no way she would be able to make it home before dark. Panic surged within her as she imagined the dangers she might face on her trek home.

Watching the people walk away from their useless vehicles and back toward where she and Tamara were standing with a group of other observers, Melissa thought about her husband and children. Her husband, Alex, worked several miles south of Melissa's office—on the way home. But she had no idea what his next move would be. They had never discussed what to do in this kind of emergency. Why would they? Who could have imagined something like this actually happening? She'd always believed that the fiction she'd read was just that. Now though, she regretted not taking the idea of this happening seriously.

Shaking away the thought, she pictured her three children. All of them were at school, but both schools were less than a mile from home. Both seventeen-year-old Jason and fifteen-year-old Emily were at the high school. Thirteen-year-old Steven was at the middle school, which was only a few blocks from home. Melissa fervently hoped they would all head straight home and not go off to friends' houses. Even so, the thought of them being at home completely on their own until she or Alex could get there was unsettling. Not because they were irresponsible—in fact they were all really good kids—but because of the chaos that would inevitably ensue when people realized that society was in the midst of a collapse.

CHAPTER 2

Alex

ALEX LOOKED through the glass wall in his office toward the reception area. The power had just gone out, but sunlight from the glass doors at the entrance to the small building let in enough light for him to see that his co-workers were beginning to gather in the small foyer. He stood from his desk and joined them.

"Wonder how long it will be out," someone said.

"Probably not long," Greg said.

Alex hoped he was right. He had a lot of work to do. As a product development engineer for a laser company, he kept extremely busy. He wondered if the power was out at Melissa's office. Her building was in downtown Salt Lake, several miles north of where he was. It seemed unlikely they would both have a power outage at the same time. Not on such a clear spring day. Still, he wanted to ask her. He took his phone out of the pocket of his dark gray slacks and tilted it up like he always did to wake it, but the screen remained black. He pressed the power button. Nothing happened.

"That's weird," he murmured. No one heard him over their own conversation. He pressed the buttons to turn the phone off, waited several seconds, then long-pressed the power button to turn it back on. Nothing. Last time he'd checked, his battery had been nearly full. He looked at the people around him who were busy chatting and joking. "My phone won't turn on," he said.

Greg shifted his eyes to Alex. "Battery's probably dead."

"I don't think that's it." Although he didn't want to consider what it might actually be. "Does yours work?" He fervently hoped it would.

Greg pulled his phone out of his pocket and tapped the screen. Nothing happened. He pressed the power button. Still nothing. "Huh."

This got everyone else trying. Not a single phone worked.

Oh crap, he thought as mounting dread swept over him.

It was becoming increasingly clear that Alex's worse fear was being realized. And he had no way to get in contact with Melissa who would have been affected as well. Did she realize it was an EMP? If so, what would she do? Should he go to her office? Should he go home where the kids would, hopefully, be safely waiting?

Slight panic began to build inside him. He needed to protect his family. That was the kind of thing he did. But how could he when he was miles away from them and completely unsure what they were all doing in this situation? Because he knew if this was an EMP, cell phones and electricity wouldn't be the only things that had stopped working. Most cars wouldn't run either. At least that had always been the theory. But theories were sometimes wrong. Often wrong, in fact.

Fresh hope surged inside him. Not waiting to see what anyone else's theory might be, he walked away from the group and toward the glass doors. He stopped in front of them, waiting for them to automatically slide open like they usually did. They stayed in place.

Duh. The power was out. They wouldn't open without power. Annoyed with himself for not thinking straight, he strode back through the main space and down a short hallway toward the side door exit. It was extremely dark in the hallway, but he knew his way and had no trouble reaching the exit. He pushed the door open. Sunlight streamed through the doorway. He squeezed his eyes closed against the sudden brightness, then walked out into the parking lot, going straight to his truck. He took his keys out of his pocket and pressed the unlock button on his key fob then grabbed the handle on the driver's door. It was still locked. The key fob hadn't worked. Not a good sign. Going old school, he inserted his key into the lock and turned it, then opened the door. He slid inside, then jammed his key into the ignition, a sliver of hope dancing inside him. He turned the key to start his truck. Nothing. Not even a click. Swearing quietly, he tried again. Then, once more. It was dead. Completely and utterly dead.

He lifted his gaze to see that his co-workers had all

flooded out of the building. They were going to their cars as well. These were not stupid people. They had obviously figured out the same thing Alex had. Somehow, an EMP had taken out the power grid and everything else that ran on computer chips. Which was just about everything in today's world.

Concern growing, Alex got out of his truck and looked around, hopeful that someone's car would be old enough to be immune.

The sound of an engine starting reached his ears. Heart stuttering, he spun around. Colton's classic Mustang had started right up.

Yes!

Alex hurried over to him, as did everyone else whose cars were now nothing but huge chunks of metal. About fifteen people now surrounded Colton's Mustang, all wearing smiles of relief.

"Can I get a lift?" someone asked.

"Me too," another person said.

"Same here," a third person said.

"I can only fit three people," Colton said, his expression apologetic. "Four, if we really cram in. I live in Ogden. Who else lives that way?"

Ogden was in the opposite direction of Alex's house. Like, an hour away from Alex and Melissa's house. And that was in normal traffic. If this was an EMP, the Interstate would be clogged with stalled cars, which meant getting home from Ogden could take hours.

Then again, walking would take a heck of a lot longer than that.

Maybe Alex could get Colten to drop him off at Melissa's office. At least that way he could protect her as she headed home. But what if she managed to get a ride from someone at her work? Someone who had a car that was functional? That would put him that much farther from home.

Still, it was worth a try.

Alex opened his mouth to make his suggestion, but four people who either lived in Ogden or on the way there were already climbing into Colton's Mustang. And two other people were getting angry that there wasn't room for them.

Crap! Alex thought as he shook his head in frustration. *Now what?*

CHAPTER 3

Melissa

As Melissa imagined people doing whatever they wanted because the authorities were either overwhelmed or busy caring for their own families, a sharp sense of fear rolled through her chest. Even more frightening, when food ran out—which was sure to happen rapidly—and people realized the food delivery system had been terminated and no more food would be coming, there was no telling what desperate acts people would be willing to commit to keep themselves and their families fed.

Shoving those worries away, she tried to focus on the immediate problem—how to get home quickly and safely. It was now three o'clock, and since it was late March, there were about four hours of daylight left. At least it wasn't too cold that day—about forty degrees—although once the sun set it would get a lot colder.

"What are you going to do?" Tamara asked, her forehead creased with worry.

Melissa looked around at the other people, who looked as perplexed as she felt. "I'm not sure what to do. It's kind of late in the day. Do you think we could make it home before dark?"

"What kind of pace do you think we could keep?"

"On the treadmill I can walk almost four miles an hour, but that's my upper limit and that's for about fifteen minutes." She frowned. "And that's wearing comfortable shoes. So realistically, I can probably go about two and a half to three miles an hour for a long time." She grimaced. "Maybe." And that was if they didn't run into any trouble.

Tamara looked thoughtful. "So... it would take you about seven hours to get home and me about five."

Melissa sighed. "Yeah. It will be way past dark before we make it all the way home." As her imagination conjured up all kinds of nighttime dangers in a situation where there was no electricity, no cell phones, no working vehicles—and probably no law enforcement—her heart began to pound. "The thought of being out after dark freaks me out."

"What about Alex? What if you met up with him?"

"That would be a great, but I don't know what he's going to do or which roads he'll be taking. And no way to contact him." Melissa shook her head. "I can't count on him as a walking companion." Melissa paused. "What about your husband? What do you think he'll do?" Tamara was thirty and had one child, a six-year-old daughter.

"Well, Rich only has to commute a few miles to his job, so it won't take him long to get home. And he's usually the one to pick up Abby from school, so I would expect that he'll make sure she's safe. But that doesn't stop me from worrying."

"Me too. My kids are older though, so hopefully they'll go straight home from school." Sighing with frustration and worry, Melissa ran her fingers through her shoulder-length, brown hair. "I just want to get home. Now."

"The more time we stand around talking," Tamara said, "the less time we have before dark."

Nodding, Melissa looked at the people standing in the parking lot, who were talking in small groups, which gave her an idea. "Hey, everybody," she called out. Everyone turned to look at her. "I'm sure we all want to get home, and I was thinking, maybe we could get in groups according to the general area where we live and maybe walk together. You know, safety in numbers?"

When everyone nodded, Melissa felt the knot of worry in her chest begin to loosen. As people shouted out where they lived, groups quickly formed. Melissa smiled at Tamara as she stayed in Melissa's group.

"I don't live quite as far as you, but we both need to go the same way," Tamara said with a smile.

Melissa appraised the other people in her group, a feeling of warmth spreading through her chest. These were all people she worked with and cared about, and she knew they would do all they could to help each other reach home safely.

As she studied the four other people in her group, she

silently catalogued their strengths and weaknesses: Rob, mid-thirties, in reasonably good shape, smart and a problem solver but liked to be in charge. Dillon, mid-twenties, strong, but still somewhat immature. John, late forties and in poor health, but a really nice guy. And then there was Tamara, Melissa's good friend. Eight years younger than Melissa, she was in great shape and someone Melissa cared about. She was glad to have her in her group.

"What now?" Tamara asked.

"We should take food and water with us," John said. "It's going to be a long walk."

Worried how he would do with so much physical exertion, Melissa regarded him. Overweight, John seemed to have trouble just walking around the office without getting out of breath. Though worried, Melissa pushed it aside. They would all just have to manage the best they could.

"Don't most of us have snacks at our desks?" Rob asked.

"I know I do," Melissa said.

Several others agreed.

"Let's gather all the snacks and water bottles we can and meet back out here," Rob said.

"Does anyone have a backpack or something to carry them with?" Melissa asked.

Two in the group raised their hands.

"Bring those too," Rob said.

The five of them walked toward the building and Melissa heard some of the other groups discussing the same strategy.

As she descended the stairwell, Melissa held on to the railing. "I can't see a thing," she said to Tamara, who she assumed was nearby, although she couldn't be sure.

"Just be careful," Tamara said from behind her.

Feeling her way, Melissa reached her cubicle. After putting on her sweater—even if she warmed up while walking, she knew she would need it eventually—she opened the cabinet above her desk and stuck her hand in, patting the space until she touched an item she knew was a box of protein bars. She grabbed the other items, which included a bag of dried fruit and a half-eaten box of pop-tarts. She took out her purse, which was basically a small backpack, and placed the food inside, then grabbed the half-full water bottle that was sitting next to her computer monitor.

"How are you coming along, Tamara?" she asked into the darkness.

"I'm ready," Tamara's answered. "How about you?"

"I just want to top off my water bottle."

A moment later Tamara entered Melissa's cubicle and they moved carefully through the darkness toward the drinking fountain Melissa always used to fill her water bottle. But when she pressed the lever, nothing happened.

"Oh," she said, feeling stupid. "I guess this runs on electricity." She turned around, trying to figure out where to go. "I'm going to try the sink in the break room."

A few moments later she had her water bottle under the faucet, filling it.

"I wonder how long the water will work," Tamara said.

"Why wouldn't it?"

"Doesn't the water company use electricity to pump the water?"

She hadn't thought about that. Fresh worry made Melissa's insides clench. What would happen if people couldn't get water? She didn't even want to consider that. Fortunately, they had a decent amount of water stored at their house, thanks to the suggestion of their next-door neighbor, Stan, who was into prepping.

"I guess I'm ready to go," Melissa said, but she felt more unprepared than she ever had in her life.

CHAPTER 4
Alex

Alex watched the Mustang disappear in the distance, then he turned and looked at the others who had been left behind. Some were grumbling that they hadn't been able to go in the only working vehicle, while others turned and plodded back toward the building.

For a moment, Alex was undecided about what to do. Head toward Melissa's office or toward home? He couldn't do both. They were in opposite directions.

"What are you going to do?" Jack, a man who worked in Alex's office, asked him.

Alex shook his head, his lips flat. "My wife's in Salt Lake, but my kids are in Sandy. What about you?"

Jack looked off in the distance like the answer lay somewhere just out of reach. Then he turned to Alex with a frown. "Guess I'm going to walk home."

"Which is where, exactly?"

"I'm all the way down in American Fork."

That was miles south of where Alex lived. Alex chewed on the inside of his lip as he contemplated his options. He hated the idea of Melissa trying to make her way home on her own, but with multiple options of streets for her to follow, he had no idea which way she would go. Then he thought about his three children, all on their own.

Clenching his jaw in frustration, he exhaled through his nose, then came to a decision. "I'll walk with you, but I want to take Ninth East." That would probably be the shortest path to take him home. And with any luck, maybe he would somehow run in to Melissa. Still, he knew it would be out of the way for Jack.

Shaking his head, Jack said, "I was thinking State Street."

State Street was nine blocks west of where Alex wanted to go—too far out of the way. "Thought you'd say that."

Jack chuckled.

Knowing there would be safety in numbers, Alex decided to try to persuade his friend. "You know, State Street's going to be a more dangerous route than Ninth."

"Why do you say that?"

"More shops along there. Don't you think they'll be hit by looters? Could get dicey."

"True, but Ninth is nine blocks east of where I need to go."

Alex nodded. "Tell you what. Let's take Seventh East. Kind of a compromise."

Jack laughed. "It's tempting, but I'll take my chances on State Street."

Though it would have been nice to have backup, Alex understood Jack's reluctance to go out of his way. "All right." Really though, Alex would have backup. Just a different kind. He brushed his hand against his right hip, a grim smile lifting his lips as he felt the hard bulge of his Glock 19. He was glad he was carrying today. He often left his weapon at home, but after all the craziness of the Covid pandemic and the civil unrest that seemed to be a constant around the country, he felt a little safer knowing he was armed. He'd tried to get Melissa to carry—she'd gotten her Conceal Carry Permit—but she hadn't felt the need, even though she had a small pistol, a .380.

Wondering if Jack carried, Alex asked, "You armed?"

"Always," Jack said with a grin as he adjusted the pack on his back.

Rather surprised—Jack had never seemed like the kind of person who was into guns—Alex raised his eyebrows.

"You?" Jack asked, his forehead furrowed like he doubted it.

"Yeah," Alex said, his expression neutral.

"Really?" Jack's tone held a note of disbelief.

"Why so surprised?"

"Just didn't peg you as the type."

This brought on a hearty laugh. "I thought the same thing about you."

Shaking his head, Jack chuckled. "You think you know

someone, and then they surprise you." He pursed his lips. "Guess you never know about people."

This was truer than Alex wanted to consider, although he knew he had to. Because now that society was on the brink of collapse, people would become more unpredictable than ever, putting everyone in danger. "Well," Alex said, "Best of luck to you."

Jack nodded. "You too." With a nod, Jack turned and walked toward the road.

Shaking his head but smiling, Alex decided to gather a few supplies before he started his trek. He didn't have a backpack, but he knew at least one of the people who'd gotten a ride with Colton usually had one. Alex went back inside the building, then into the man's office before rummaging through his desk. It didn't take long to find what he was looking for. Smiling tightly in triumph, Alex carried the backpack to the break room, which was illuminated by the sun streaming in through a large window on one wall. First, he dumped out the contents to see what was already in there. A flashlight, a small first aid kit, a nice pocketknife, a couple of books, and a few other odds and ends that Alex didn't find useful.

Guess he didn't want to take the time to grab his pack and chance losing his spot in the Mustang, Alex thought. Well, it was a huge blessing to Alex to have this gear. He put the items he wanted to take back in the pack, then set six bottles of water inside. Next, he liberated a dozen granola bars and several other snacks. Who knew how long it would take to get home? He would need the energy the food would provide.

As soon as he was done, he walked out of the building and into the parking lot. Four of his coworkers stood in a group. Alex knew all of them lived either west or north of Salt Lake, so not in the direction he was headed. Alex gave them a wave, then he walked to the nearest cross-street and turned south.

CHAPTER 5

Melissa

When Melissa walked outside again, she squinted against the bright sunlight. After taking her backpack purse off of her shoulders, she removed a pair of sunglasses, put them on her face, then slung the backpack purse over both shoulders. Walking with Tamara to rejoin their group, Melissa saw that one person was missing. "Where's John?"

"He's still getting his stuff," Rob said.

"I hate to be the one to point this out," Dillon said, "but he's really going to slow us down."

Melissa frowned. Though she'd thought the same thing, she didn't feel right about leaving John behind.

"What are you suggesting?" Tamara asked.

"I want to get home to my family as fast as possible, and like it or not, he's going to make it take twice as long. I don't know about you," Dillon said, looking directly at Tamara, "but

I'd rather get home before it gets too dark. If we have to go John's pace, there's no way that will happen."

"What are you saying?" Melissa asked. "That we should just leave him here?"

Dillon shrugged, but his thoughts were clear. Leave John behind.

"That wouldn't be right," Melissa said. "He's as much a part of this group as any of us."

"Sorry," John said a moment later as he came bustling out of the door, already a bit out of breath, a backpack on his shoulders.

Melissa shifted her gaze to Dillon, who looked away from John and rolled his eyes at Rob. Rob's lips were pressed into a straight line.

Not wanting to get bogged down in this early dispute, Melissa said, "Let's get going."

The five of them crossed the parking lot and made a left, heading toward 700 East. The first thing Melissa noticed were the cars stopped in the middle of the street. Some had people sitting inside, but many had been abandoned. As they walked, she saw small clumps of people standing outside of other buildings, talking.

"Wonder how long it will take them to figure out what happened," Rob murmured.

Melissa turned to look at him, then shrugged. "Maybe we should tell them."

"We can't stop and talk to everyone," Rob said with a scowl. "That will slow us down even more."

True as that was, what if more people could join their group? Wouldn't that be a good thing? Without asking how everyone else felt about it, Melissa said, "Just give me a minute." Then she trotted off to a group of seven people—four women and three men.

The people looked her way as she approached. She smiled. "Hey."

They smiled in return. A woman who looked like she was in her forties and was dressed in a skirt and blouse stepped forward. "Do you know what's going on?" She held up her cell phone. "I mean, the power went out, but our phones aren't working either."

Melissa explained her EMP theory. After listening to their shocked responses, Melissa gestured to her group. Rob's arms were crossed over his chest and Dillon had his hands on his hips. Ignoring their obvious impatience, Melissa swiveled back to face the people she was talking to. "We're walking home. Heading south. Do any of you live that way?"

Two of the men and one of the women said they did.

"If you want to join us," Melissa said, "you can."

"Sounds good," said one of the men, who looked like he was in his forties and seemed fit. He wore dress slacks and a button up shirt.

The other man, who wore a suit, nodded. "Yeah. I'll come." He was older, maybe late fifties.

The woman glanced at the high heels on her feet. "Not exactly the best shoes for walking."

Melissa nodded. "Still, what other choice do you have?"

The woman eyed the people who hadn't spoken yet. "I'm going to stay here. See if the power comes back on."

Holding back a sigh—no point in trying to convince her it wasn't coming back on—Melissa nodded. "All right. Well, good luck to you."

The men who had been with the woman tossed her a smile, then walked with Melissa toward her group. When they reached them, Melissa noticed that Rob's lips were twisted into a deep frown. Ignoring him, she turned to the two men, introducing everyone from her group.

The man in his mid-fifties nodded. "Nice to meet everyone. I'm Curtis." He smiled at Melissa. "Thanks for including me."

"Yeah, thanks," the other man said. "I'm Tyler."

"Let's get going," Rob grumbled.

Melissa looked at Tamara, who seemed fine with the stop, and shook her head.

As they walked, Melissa asked the two newcomers what they did.

"We're both attorneys," Tyler, the younger man said. "What about you?"

"I'm a project manager," Melissa said, remembering the PowerPoint she'd been working on. If this was truly an EMP, then the PowerPoint wouldn't matter. Nothing she'd been working on would. All that would matter was surviving. The thought was sobering.

The group was silent, everyone lost in their own thoughts.

Soon, they reached 700 East. They turned right—south—and continued on.

As they walked, they passed through a residential area. Some people were outside talking to neighbors, but everyone was calm. That gave Melissa hope that they wouldn't run in to too much craziness. Then again, did people understand what had happened? She kind of doubted it.

They kept plodding along, passing house after house and stopped car after stopped car. Some people were milling about. Others were walking like they'd given up on getting their cars to start and needed to get somewhere. Several people had children with them. Melissa felt sorry for those people. It was hard enough to walk a long distance with only herself to worry about. If she had little ones too, that would make it so much more difficult.

They passed a park. It was too early in the year for the leaves to bud, but the trees were beautiful, nevertheless.

Melissa's right baby toe was rubbing against her shoe. Worried that she would get a blister so early in her long trek, she tried wiggling her toes from time to time in the hopes that would keep a blister from forming.

An hour later, the discomfort on Melissa's right baby toe was becoming unbearable. She knew she'd gotten a blister from her stupid boots—stylish, but not meant for long walks. Which is also when she saw a shopping center.

Hoping against hope that she would be able to fix the issue with her feet, she turned to the group. "I need to find some comfortable shoes." She grimaced. "My feet are killing me."

"I could use some different shoes too," Tamara admitted.

Glad she wasn't the only one, Melissa said, "Maybe one of the stores in here has shoes."

Expecting the others—or at least Dillon and Rob—to look annoyed, she skimmed over their faces, but everyone seemed like they were ready for a short break.

"Maybe I can get more water," John said, holding up his nearly empty water bottle.

Then Tyler, the lawyer who had joined their group, gestured with his chin toward the shopping center. "We may have a problem."

CHAPTER 6

Alex

Alex had barely begun heading east on 3300 South when he saw two men fighting in the street. There were numerous cars in all six lanes, all dead, all blocking the road. Which made Alex wonder how far Colton and his passengers had gotten in the Mustang. Not that he would turn down a ride, but still. Couldn't have gotten far. Not if all the roads were like this.

It seemed as if the men were fighting over the fact that one had run into the other. Didn't they know their cars were worthless now?

One of the men turned and stormed away. Was the fight over? The man opened the passenger door to what must have been his car, leaned in for several moments, then stood and swiveled around to face the man he'd been fighting with. Half a second later, he raised a gun at the other man and opened fire. The man he was shooting at collapsed to the ground.

With nowhere to take cover, Alex dove to the sidewalk. The shooter, who was about twenty yards from Alex, strode over to the man he'd shot and stood over him, his gun pointed at him, his face a mask of fury. Alex rested his hand on his Glock, his gaze riveted to the scene.

The shooter lifted his eyes and glared at the people watching him before pointing his gun at first one person, then another while yelling, "You got a problem? Huh?"

With wide eyes, people shook their heads and held up their hands to show they were harmless. The shooter finally lowered his gun, tucking it into the back of his jeans before stalking away.

Removing his hand from his Glock, Alex slowly got up, his eyes on the shooter. Once the man reached the corner and began disappearing from view, Alex began to relax slightly, although he was on high alert for the next incident that was sure to occur.

Shocked that a cold-blooded murder had occurred right in the streets of Salt Lake City, right in front of him, he shook his head in disbelief. Even more stunning, no law enforcement came to the scene, and of course no one could call for help since all cell phones had been turned into colorful bricks.

Taking several moments to gather himself, Alex's thoughts went to Melissa. What was she facing on her travels home? Was she safe? Was she all alone? That thought sent a zing of deep fear coursing through his chest. If only he knew where she was, he would go directly to her. Severely missing his iPhone and the Find My app, which would tell him exactly where she was at the tap of the screen, he audibly sighed and continued on his way, heading east toward 900 East.

"Hey, mister," a man said as he approached Alex several minutes later. The shopping cart filled with random items as well as his dirty clothing pegged the man as homeless.

Alex turned to him with a frown. He didn't have time for this.

"Hey," the man said, "hey, what's going on? Why'd all the cars stop?"

Slightly less annoyed that the man was only asking for information, Alex said, "Ever heard of an EMP?"

The man's eyebrows bunched. "A what?"

"EMP. Electromagnetic Pulse."

His expression smoothed out. "Oh yeah. I heard of that." The man's eyes slid to the pack on Alex's back. "What'cha got in there?"

Okay. Here it came. Alex began walking. The man hurried to keep up.

"Got any food in there? I sure am hungry."

Alex considered the ramifications of what the man was asking. In normal times he wouldn't have minded giving the man some of his food. But these weren't normal times. And this wouldn't be the last time he would be faced with someone asking for what he had. In some cases, he was sure, people would demand what he had. Especially as things became more desperate. The thought pushed him to quicken his pace. He needed to get home to his children—and pray that Melissa would make it home safely.

"Hey," the man shouted. "Hey. Don't walk away from me."

Getting annoyed now, Alex noticed several people watching the exchange. These were people whose cars had died. For some reason they were staying with their vehicles as if they were waiting for a fleet of tow trucks to rescue them.

Shaking his head, Alex kept walking. Next thing he knew, the homeless man was grabbing at his backpack, trying to rip it off his shoulders. Alex spun around and shoved the guy, knocking him down.

"Why'd you do that?" the man asked, his tone bewildered.

"Back off," Alex said, his tone sharp and sure.

Scowling, the man pointed at Alex. "You better watch out. You don't got no car to hide in now."

The truth of the man's words hit Alex in the gut. He was right. Alex was on foot. No car windows to roll up. No car to speed off in. And he was by himself. Sure, he had his Glock, but he was no action hero. If he got jumped by several people, he wasn't sure what his odds would be.

Tamping down that worry, he began walking, increasing his pace as much as he could without breaking into a jog. He needed to conserve his energy. He had a good fifteen miles to go. Not a lot, but it would take him at least four hours—if he could keep up this pace, which he knew he wouldn't be able to do. He wasn't in *that* great of shape. Plus, he was sure to run into obstacles.

Keeping his head on a swivel, he moved forward, determined to get home as quickly as he could.

CHAPTER 7

Melissa

EAGER TO GIVE her blistered toe relief, Melissa squinted toward the far end of the shopping center where Tyler was looking. That's when she saw frenzied activity as clumps of people pushed their way into stores while others carried out armloads of items.

"What's happening?" John asked, one hand raised to shade his eyes.

"Looks like looters," Tyler said.

Melissa's heart sank. If people were already starting to take advantage of the power being out, then they must have realized this was more than a run-of-the-mill outage and that it was something more permanent. Something that would send them back to the Stone Age.

"Should we wait?" asked Tamara.

The throbbing in Melissa's foot made the decision for her. "No. I've got to get a pair of sneakers or I'm going to hate life while we walk home."

"All right," Tyler began, "here's what we're going to do."

Rob put his hand up. "Hold on. Who put you in charge?"

Melissa sighed, but kept quiet. She had to be the referee at home, she wasn't about to be one with grown men. They would have to figure this out themselves. She just hoped they wouldn't take too long because she wanted to swap out her shoes and be on her way as soon as possible. The clock was ticking toward sunset. Melissa didn't want to think about the dangers she—and the rest of her group—would face once the sun had gone down and complete darkness had cloaked the night.

Tyler frowned at Rob. "You want to be in charge? Fine. What's your plan to get what we need when looters are everywhere?"

Rob scowled, then his lips compressed before he finally said, "We blend in. Act like we're there to loot too."

"What are you saying?" Tamara asked. "That we're going to steal what we need?"

"Not if there's someone there to take payment," Rob answered.

"Uh," Melissa began, "I don't have cash. And I doubt they'll be able to take a credit card."

"I have some cash," Curtis, the other lawyer they'd added to their group, offered.

Melissa turned to him with a grateful smile. "Thank you."

He smiled in return. "No problem."

Feeling optimistic, Melissa began walking toward the row of stores. Everyone came with her. The first few stores were small restaurants. The looters were farther down. As she got closer, Melissa saw what had attracted them. A cell phone store. And right beside it was a shoe outlet store.

They passed the cell phone store with Dillon muttering, "Those phones aren't going to do them much good now."

Ignoring his comment, Melissa was focused on the shoe store. Multiple people were hustling out with boxes of shoes in their arms. She hoped they still had at least one pair in her size.

She reached the door but had to step back to get out of the way of two people running out. Once those looters had cleared the door, she crossed the threshold. Pure chaos greeted her. People were ransacking the shelves, tossing boxes and shoes everywhere. She turned to see if her group had followed her in, but just saw Tamara and Tyler, who were right behind her. Relieved to not be alone, she focused on Tamara. "What size do you wear?"

"Six and a half."

"I'm a seven. Let's hurry and see if we can find anything in our size." She shifted her gaze to Tyler. "What about you?"

He chuckled. "I'm good. I just came in to watch your backs."

Gratitude swept through her. "Thank you."

He glanced at his dress shoes. "Although I might see if there's something more comfortable while I'm in here."

"Good idea." Melissa gave Tamara a grim smile. "Let's go."

The two of them waded through the crowd, stepping over empty boxes and abandoned shoes until they reached an area with a sign that showed their shoe sizes. Melissa immediately began digging through the shelves, picking up shoes and checking the sizes listed inside. Tamara did the same. She glanced at the other people there. No one was getting violent. Yet. She turned to Tyler. "I think we'll be okay if you want to go look for shoes for yourself."

He narrowed his eyes. "You sure?"

Not really. "Yeah."

Nodding once, he said, "All right."

She watched him go, then continued digging. Finally, she found a left shoe that was her size, but she couldn't find its mate. Frustrated, but not about to be deterred, she pulled off her left boot and replaced it with the red sneaker. It fit perfectly. "Now I just need one for my left foot," she muttered.

She looked over at Tamara to see how she was doing and saw her friend putting a matching pair on her feet. Tamara scowled and looked at Melissa. "Too tight. I'm going to go to the next aisle."

Melissa nodded, then went back to her own hunt. Eventually she found a size seven for her right foot in dark blue. A single shoe. Probably the last size seven in the store. Sighing in relief, she set it on the floor beside her as she pulled off her right boot, but just as she was about to pick up the shoe to put it on, someone snatched it away.

"Hey!" she cried out, leaping to her feet to face the thief. It was a large, rough-looking man, and he was glaring at her as if he was daring her to take it back. Confused why he was grabbing a woman's shoe, and not a little afraid of what he would do if she confronted him, she gathered her courage. She *needed* that shoe. "That's my shoe."

He laughed at her, revealing perfectly straight, white teeth. Then he held up the shoe in his hand. "This one?"

Growing angry, Melissa said, "Yeah."

He laughed again, then turned and began walking away.

She dashed after him and grabbed his shirt. "Stop!"

He did stop, and then he slowly turned to face her. The laughter had evaporated from his face, replaced by a look of menace. "Don't freaking touch me, lady."

"Give me back my shoe!"

He lifted his free hand like he was going to hit her. She recoiled. Was she really going to risk getting hurt over a stupid shoe?

His lip curled as he stared at her, his eyes growing dark with rage.

She was in over her head, but when she backed up, she tripped over the mess of shoes on the floor behind her, falling on her rear end. The man pulled his foot back and Melissa braced herself for the kick she knew she wouldn't be able to avoid, but rather than swinging his leg toward her, he crumpled to the ground, the shoe dropping from his hand.

Melissa's gaze shot to the man who stood behind him, a gun in his hand, but with the butt pointing down. It was Tyler. He'd hit the man over the head with a gun. Where had he gotten the gun? Wait. Who cared? He'd saved her from getting injured or worse.

Grabbing the shoe from the floor, Melissa shoved it onto her right foot, then got to her feet, leaving her boots behind.

"Are you okay?" Tyler asked.

"Yes. Thank you." Eager to get away from the pandemonium, she turned to see if Tamara had found a pair of shoes. She had, and she was ready to go.

The trio hustled out of the store—there was no one taking payment, and clearly that wasn't the most important thing just then. When they got outside, Melissa half-expected their group to have gone on without them, but to her delight, they were all there, waiting.

John looked at Melissa's mismatched shoes and chuckled. "You found something to wear, I see."

Melissa looked down, then smiled at him. "Yep. But I only have them thanks to Tyler." She swept her gaze over Tyler. He was wearing new sneakers, but the gun was no longer visible. Obviously, he carried concealed. She was glad at least one member of their group was armed.

"What happened?" Tamara asked. "I was on the next aisle and saw you arguing with some guy, but that's all."

Melissa glanced toward the store, worried that the man Tyler had knocked out would wake up and come after them. "Let's get going and I'll tell you."

They headed back to the street with Melissa recounting what had happened, leaving out what Tyler had used to knock the man out. When she finished the story, everyone stayed quiet as they walked. Melissa's feet felt better already, and despite what had happened, she was glad they'd stopped.

"How'd you knock that guy out?" Rob asked Tyler. "I mean, did you just hit him with your fist?"

"I hit him with the butt of my gun."

"Your gun?" John asked. "You're armed too?"

Melissa's eyebrows shot up as she stopped and turned to John. "What do you mean 'too'?"

He grinned and lifted his shirt to reveal a holster on the inside of his waistband which held a handgun.

All this time she'd worked with John and had no idea he conceal carried too. Her eyes swept over the rest of her group. "Anyone else?"

"I have a permit," Curtis said, "but I don't have my weapon with me today. Unfortunately."

"No gun, but I do have this." Dillon pulled a folding knife out his front pocket and held it out for all to see, then he put it away.

Rob shook his head. "Sorry. No weapons here."

"I don't have anything either," Melissa said, regretting that she hadn't listened to her husband's advice to carry her small pistol. She'd never felt all that comfortable doing so. Now she wished she had it with her. "I have to admit," she said, "I feel safer knowing some of you are armed." Her thoughts remained on her husband. What was he doing right then?

Had he found a way home? If he was on foot, would he try to find her? She knew he would be worried about her, but she felt safe in her group and hoped he would focus on getting home to the kids. One of them needed to get home and make sure the kids were all right.

CHAPTER 8

Alex

Alex covered two blocks, and as he walked, he scanned the area. A pawn shop across the street caught his eye. A pair of men stood just outside the doors, rifles in their hands, their heads moving from side to side as they watched every person in the vicinity.

As Alex continued, he noticed that more cars in the roadway had been abandoned. People must have figured out that the cars weren't going to start no matter how much they wished they would. Consequently, more people were on foot. Many wore looks of bewilderment as they plodded toward some destination or another. Others seemed focused on getting to wherever they were going, not looking around at all. Several people stared at their phones, tapping at their screens as if they would come back to life if they just tapped on them long enough.

Glad he had a clue about what was happening, which could only give him an advantage, Alex strode onward.

He reached a corner where a car repair shop stood. A man was arguing with a mechanic, accusing him of doing something to his car. "You broke it and now it won't start!"

The mechanic gestured to the cars in the street and shouted, "Can't you see that *all* the cars are dead?"

The customer shifted toward the street, and as he scanned all of the cars stopped in the middle of the road, a deep frown grew on his face. After several long moments, he turned back to the mechanic. "Can you fix my car? Can you make it start?"

The mechanic shook his head, then turned away as if to go back inside the garage. This must have angered the customer, because he grabbed the mechanic by the arm and yanked him. The mechanic spun around and punched the customer in the jaw, knocking him to the pavement before jogging into the garage bay where he manually pulled down the large door.

Shaking his head like he was trying to shake off the hit, the customer got to his feet then stared right at Alex. "Did you see what he just did? He assaulted me."

Remembering the shooting a few blocks earlier, Alex sighed. "Be glad that's all he did."

The man's eyebrows gathered together. "What do you mean?"

Not about to take the time to explain the state of the world, Alex kept walking, calling out behind him, "If your legs work, you'd better use them to get yourself home." The man stared after Alex, clearly perplexed by his new reality.

Alex approached a strip mall, which included an electronics store. Several people appeared to be looting the place. Snorting a laugh at the ludicrousness of that, Alex shook his head.

Out of nowhere, someone tackled him, taking him to the ground. Stunned, he landed on his back. The man who had knocked him down was on top of him, but he rolled off of Alex before starting to tug at Alex's backpack. Adrenaline dumped into Alex's veins. The man who had attacked him was a little bigger than Alex, but he didn't look fit. He just looked fat.

Not about to lose his only means of food and water for the long walk home, Alex twisted his body toward the man, which tore the backpack out of the man's grip. At the same time, Alex swung his right fist up and punched the man in the kidney as hard as he could. The man grunted and fell back, giving Alex the time he needed to leap to his feet. He immediately drew his gun and pointed it at the man. "Back off!"

The man's eyes widened so much that the whites of his eyes showed. Then the man threw his hands up and slowly backed away.

Using his peripheral vision and a quick turn of his head, Alex made sure no one else was about to attack him.

"Run," Alex commanded, his tone low and menacing.

The man turned and ran. When he was a distance away, Alex lowered his weapon and slowly scrutinized the area around him. When he was satisfied that he was in the clear, he tucked his Glock back into his waist holster and forced himself to get moving despite the way his heart was jackhammering in his chest.

Dragging in a deep breath as he started to walk, he was tempted to start jogging, just to put distance between himself and the altercation. But he knew himself well enough to know that he needed to set a pace he could maintain. Working to keep his breathing even, he set a brisk pace and became more deliberate about being attuned to his surroundings. He'd gotten distracted by the things people were doing, things that had no relevance to him. He couldn't let that happen again. He was lucky the guy who'd tackled him wasn't armed himself or wasn't bigger or stronger.

At the next corner, he turned south. He'd been walking for a while but it seemed like he hadn't gotten very far at all. Frustrated, he exhaled audibly and shook his head. At this rate, by the time he got home it would be dark. He had to move faster.

A bike would be nice right about now, he thought. Too bad there weren't any in sight.

A grocery store was on his right. He noticed people coming out with carts filled to overflowing. Which made him think about what was in his pantry at home. Despite having a decent amount of food storage, right then it didn't seem like nearly enough. Not with society on the brink of collapse. By the time he got home, would there be anything left at the grocery store near his house? Because if possible, he wanted to round out what they had. With three growing teenagers and Melissa and himself, they could always use more.

Not wanting to worry about what he couldn't control, Alex slowed a bit as he swung the backpack around and pulled out a bottle of water. Taking a long pull, he drank until he was satisfied. Although the temperature was in the mid-forties, since he'd been expending energy, he wasn't chilled. In fact, the bright sun kept him warm. Figuring it had to be getting close to four o'clock, he did worry about how cold it would get once the sun went down. Last he'd checked, it was supposed to get below freezing that night.

He put the nearly empty water bottle back in his pack and continued on. Houses lined both sides of the street, but although he was in a residential area, he was on a main thoroughfare, and with all the dead cars, there were plenty of people walking.

Alex's thoughts went to Melissa. Where was she just then? Was she all right? Was she with other people or was she alone? The need to make sure she was safe was nearly overwhelming, but since he had no idea which road she had taken—or if she'd managed to get a ride or was walking—he really had no choice but to focus on getting home to the kids. Certain that Melissa would be more concerned about the kids than herself, Alex knew she would want him to concentrate on getting to them rather than finding her.

He just hoped that was a decision he wouldn't regret.

CHAPTER 9

Alex

About forty minutes later—although without his phone working and with no watch it was hard to know exactly how much time had passed—Alex figured he'd walked at least a couple of miles south on 900 East. He passed several stores before he saw a Walmart coming up on his left.

The thought of riding a bike filled his mind once again. Walmart sold bikes. And he could see people going in and out of the store, so obviously they were open for business—or people were looting. Not sure which it was, but eager for the opportunity to improve his mode of transportation, he veered off of the sidewalk and toward the entrance.

As he got closer, he saw some people running out of the store with bulging bags of goods hanging from their arms and other people carrying random items like clothing. There were even a couple of people carrying TVs.

Once he was inside, he was met with complete mayhem. People were ransacking the shelves and shoving each other to get to things first. Alex looked toward the registers. No one was stationed at any of the registers to take payment. In fact, he couldn't see any employees anywhere. Not that he blamed them. With the anarchy, who would want to try to restore order? The lights were off, of course, so the only light came from the skylights scattered all over the ceiling. It was a sunny day, so enough light streamed in to see fairly well.

Feeling less hopeful that he would find what he was looking for, he made his way toward the sporting goods section, going past the grocery side of the store where the shelves were rapidly emptying as people frantically filled their carts with food. It reminded him of the panic buying he'd seen when the country had shut down after Covid had taken hold. But this was much worse as these shoppers seemed to comprehend that once the shelves were empty, no more food would be coming. So they had to get what they could now.

Feeling an urgent need to get more for his own pantry, his whole body tensed up. As much as he would have liked to grab a bunch of food to take home, realistically he wouldn't be able to carry it for the remaining ten miles he. So, with reluctance, he walked right past the food that was left on the shelves and went directly to the sporting goods section.

When he got to the place where bikes were sold and didn't see a single bike, he was extremely disappointed though not at all surprised. Huffing a loud exhale, he shook his head, then turned and made his way back to the front of the store.

No one accosted him—they were too focused on what they could take—so he was able to leave the store without incident.

He had walked another mile along 900 East when he saw a woman riding a bike, coming in his general direction. As she got closer, she made him think of Melissa. Even though he hadn't found a bike to ride, maybe his wife had been able to. Maybe she would even be home when he got there. Imagining walking through his front door and finding her safely there, Alex felt his body relax. Until he saw a man jump at the woman on the bike, knocking her and the bike to the ground. The woman screamed.

Without thinking twice, Alex raced the short distance to where the woman was lying on the ground. The man was lifting the bike, ready to steal it, when Alex got there. Without hesitating, Alex lifted his leg and nailed the man in the back with the bottom of his shoe. With a loud *Oomph!* the man released the bike and tumbled to the pavement.

A moment later the man regained his breath, getting to his feet and turning to Alex with fury burning in his eyes. The woman, who was holding her ankle, scooted out of the way.

"You want some of this?" the man shouted, his eyes blazing.

Though he didn't want to have to keep drawing on people, it did seem to be the quickest way to make them back down. So, Alex reached into his waist holster and pulled out his gun, but rather than aim it at the man, he used both hands to hold it in the low ready position. "Move along and I won't have to shoot you." He really didn't want to shoot anyone, but he would defend himself and his family if needed. He would even defend a stranger if it came to that.

The man's hands went up as his eyes flared. "I don't want no trouble, mister." He glanced at the bike and licked his lips.

"Leave it," Alex commanded.

Visibly swallowing, the man nodded, then turned and sprinted away.

Alex tucked his gun back in his holster, then his eyes slid to the bike on the ground. He could pick it up, get on it, and be home in less than an hour. It was like an answer to a prayer. Except, was it really? How could he take it with the woman who owned it right there on the ground, clearly injured?

"Thank you," she said from behind him.

Pulled from his thoughts, Alex turned and faced her. "Are you okay?"

Her eyes went to her ankle, then back to him. "I hurt my ankle. I don't..." she shook her head. "I don't think I can ride now."

"How far do you have to go?"

"Not far. Maybe half a mile?"

He chewed on his bottom lip as he considered what he should do. If this was Melissa, Alex would want someone to help her. Not leave her in the street. Only problem was, the woman was headed in the wrong direction. If he helped her get home, that would give him an extra mile to travel—half a mile to her place, then half a mile back to where they'd started. Still, helping her was the right thing to do. Even if society was falling apart, that didn't mean he was going to suddenly change into a person who never cared about others.

He reached out a hand to the woman. "I can help you get home."

Hope filled her eyes. "Really? You'd do that?"

"Of course."

She clasped her hand in his and got to her feet, favoring her right ankle. "I'm not sure how we're going to do this," she said. "Get me and the bike home."

"We'll make it work."

She smiled. "If you say so."

"Maybe," Alex began as he mulled over the problem, "use the bike as kind of a crutch. I'll hold on to it from the other side to keep it steady."

She nodded. "Okay. I think that will work." She paused a beat. "I'm Cassie, by the way."

"Alex."

"Nice to meet you, Alex."

They slowly began making their way in the direction she'd been going, which was when Alex realized that at this pace it was going to put him at least an hour behind. Suppressing a sigh, he kept walking.

"I really appreciate you coming to my rescue," she said. "I mean, not only helping me now, which is amazing, but keeping that jerk from stealing my bike."

Shame that he'd considered, even for a moment, taking her bike, washed over him. "You're welcome."

"So," she said as she struggled along, "do you know what's

going on? I mean, my cell phone won't work and all the cars seem to be dead." She gestured to the cars parked haphazardly in the road.

Alex explained his EMP theory.

Cassie's eyes went wide. "Oh no!"

They discussed what the ramifications might be, then they were both quiet for a while before she asked, "Where were you headed?"

Feeling time slipping away, Alex said, "Home. Which is in Sandy."

She glanced at him, then her forehead furrowed. "I, uh, I have a spare bike at my house. You're welcome to take it."

Alex's eyebrows shot up as his head jerked in her direction. "Really?"

Her face lit up at his reaction. "Yes. It's the least I can do to thank you. And it'll get you home a lot faster than walking."

"Yeah it will. That would be awesome." Now *that* was an answer to his prayers. One he hadn't seen coming and one he could feel good about. Because if he'd just taken her bike and left her on the side of the road, that would have been the first step in being the person he had no desire to become.

When they finally arrived at Cassie's house, Alex helped her inside, then manually opened the garage door, after which he brought her bike in. She stood in the doorway leading from the garage to her house.

"That's the one you can take," she said as she pointed to a

dark gray men's bike leaning against the wall. "I think the tires are full."

Alex squeezed each tire. They were solid, and the bike was in great shape. He turned to her with a grin. "I really appreciate this."

She smiled. "It's my brothers. He recently got a new one and asked me to handle selling this. Hadn't gotten around to it yet."

Chuckling, Alex said, "I'm glad you didn't."

She laughed. "Me too."

Now that he had a faster way to get home, Alex was eager to get going. He told Cassie goodbye and wished her luck, then off he went. As soon as he reached 900 East, he hesitated. Should he head north and try to find Melissa? Now that he was on a bike, it wouldn't take nearly as long to search for her.

Then he pictured the shelves at the Walmart emptying so rapidly. If he made it home in the next hour, he could take the kids with him to the closest grocery store and try to stock up.

As desperate as he was to get to Melissa, he knew what she would want him to do. Go home. Get to the kids. Get provisions. Besides, she might already be home.

With a deep sigh, he turned his bike south and began pedaling.

As Alex sped along, he passed many, many people on foot. Beyond grateful to Cassie, he couldn't hold back his smile as the tires ate away the miles, and before long he reached his neighborhood. Exhaling a loud sigh of relief, he turned onto his street. A couple of his neighbors were outside talking to each other. He waved to them and they smiled and returned his greeting. Then his house came into view.

Heart pounding with anticipation at being reunited with his family, he angled the bike up his driveway, stopping once he reached the front porch. He hopped off, then, after leaning the bike against one of the pillars on the porch, he twisted the doorknob. It was locked. Was no one home, or were the kids —and Melissa?—just taking precautions? With eagerness, he took his keys out of his pocket and unlocked the door. A moment later he stepped inside.

"Melissa?" he called out. "Kids? Anyone home?"

"Dad!" Fifteen-year-old Emily said as she ran down the stairs and flung herself into his arms.

Never so happy to see his children, Alex hugged her tight. A moment later seventeen-year-old Jason and thirteen-year-old Steven joined them. Alex pulled all of them into a group hug. Which was when he realized that Melissa wasn't there.

CHAPTER 10

Alex

"Where's Mom?" Steven asked.

Holding back a frown, Alex couldn't stop the worry from creasing his brow. "I'm sure she's on her way home."

"Wait," Emily said, her forehead furrowed, "you don't know?"

Jason tilted his head like he thought his sister was being dumb. "It's not like he could call her."

Emily swiveled to face Jason with a scowl. "I know that. I'm not an idiot. It's just..." She turned back to Alex. "You guys have a plan though, right?"

Alex only wished that they did. Even though an EMP hitting their area wasn't something he'd ever really thought would happen, earthquakes were a reality. Yet he and Melissa had never discussed what they would do if they couldn't drive their cars home.

"No," Alex said, his tone filled with self-accusation. "We don't."

Didn't do any good to regret it now. All they could do was pray Melissa would get home safely. He thought about his own journey home. Despite a few dicey moments, overall it hadn't been too dangerous. He clung to that memory now.

"I'm sure she'll be fine," he said to reassure himself as much has his kids. "In the meantime, there are a lot of things we need to do."

"We already filled a bunch of containers with water," Steven said with a grin.

Impressed, Alex lifted his eyebrows. "Really? What made you think of that?"

Jason gave his younger brother a gentle shove. "As much as Steven would like you to think he's a genius, it was actually Stan from next door. He came over to check on us, and when he found out you and Mom weren't home yet, he suggested we fill whatever containers we could."

Pleased that his neighbor had done that, although not surprised—they had great neighbors—Alex smiled. "That's awesome."

"He said he thinks this power outage isn't temporary," Steven added. "He said he thinks it's an EMP. Is that true, Dad?"

Heart sinking to know that this was their new reality and that his children would have to face a rough life now, Alex couldn't stop his lips from tugging downward as he slowly nodded. "Yeah. That's my theory as well."

"So," Emily said, her eyes tight with worry, "what does that mean? Like, how is that going to affect us?"

He shifted his attention to his only daughter, then glanced at Jason and Steven as well before focusing back on her. Not wanting to fill them with the despair that was beginning to grow within him, he said, "Honestly, I don't know exactly what it's going to look like, but I do know that we need to do some things now to prepare for what might be coming."

"Like what?" Steven asked.

Alex pictured the grocery shelves emptying at the Walmart where he'd tried to get a bike. "We need to get what food we can while it's still on the shelves."

Jason nodded knowingly. "Like at the beginning of the Covid pandemic."

"Just like that." *But worse*, he didn't add.

"But the cars don't work, right?" Steven asked.

"That's right. So, we'll have to walk. And we'll push the carts home." Assuming they were able to get enough groceries to need carts. There were two grocery stores about a mile away. Not too far at all.

"How will you pay for it?" Emily asked. "I mean, without electricity they won't take a credit card, right?"

"Probably not," Alex said, grateful he had a solution. "But this was one thing Mom and I did right. We put some cash aside in our safe. I'll grab that. Hopefully it will be enough to get what we need."

Alex went into the master bedroom, setting the backpack he'd been carrying for hours onto his bed. Next, he changed into jeans and a long-sleeved shirt, making sure to transfer his inside-the-waistband holster and Glock 19 to his new attire, then he put on sneakers before going into his closet where he kept his safe. After grabbing a flashlight, he flicked it on to illuminate the safe's keypad. He punched in the safe's code, but nothing happened, which was when he realized the EMP had taken out that control. With a shake of his head, he sighed, then dug around in the upper closet shelf until he came up with the backup key he kept hidden. Using that, he opened the safe, pausing to scan his collection of firearms. He didn't have as many guns as some people he knew, but he had a decent assortment.

After counting out a sizable amount of cash, which he stuffed in his pocket, he locked the safe, putting the key where Melissa knew where to find it, and went back downstairs. Minutes later, he and the kids were hoofing it to one of the two grocery stores. These were large, chain stores, so Alex hoped they wouldn't be completely picked over yet. And that they were actually open.

Ten minutes later one of the stores came into view. Alex immediately saw that there were as many cars parked in the lot as normal, but none were moving. A handful of people were exiting the store carrying bags filled with food. At least that meant the store still had some things to buy. Several more were hurrying inside. Then Alex spotted an older vehicle pulling into the lot.

"Hey," Steven said as he pointed at the car, "how come *that* car's working? I thought the EMP killed all the cars."

The car parked a short distance away from the store entrance and two men got out, both with pistols clearly visible on their hips. Well, Alex was armed too, and he expected that many more would be openly carrying now as well.

"Older cars still work," Alex said in answer to his son, thinking of Colton's Mustang at the office, wondering if they'd all made it home. "The EMP only affects computer components. Older cars don't have those."

"We should've bought that sweet '69 Camaro," Jason said with a smirk.

Alex laughed as he pictured the car his son had seen for sale on the side of the road a few months back. "Yeah. If only we'd known what was coming."

They began crossing the parking lot, and as they got closer to the store entrance, Alex said, "I want each of you to grab a cart and fill it with whatever you think we can use. Don't get anything that can spoil, so stick to the inner aisles. Emily will stay with me, but you boys go by yourselves. We'll meet near the registers. Let's try to take no more than fifteen minutes." He looked at each child in turn. Jason looked determined, Emily seemed anxious, but Steven was grinning like this was a game. That was fine. As long as he completed his task, Alex was happy for him to think of it however he wanted.

A few moments later they reached the door.

An employee stood just inside. "Cash only," he said to Alex. "To speed things up, we're charging by the cart. Three hundred dollars per."

Yikes! Good thing Alex had enough money for each of them to fill a cart.

Alex nodded. "Okay. Thanks."

Only about a dozen shopping carts remained. Wearing a grim expression, he gestured with his head toward the carts. "Let's go."

To their credit, the kids didn't hesitate, each one grabbing a cart. The boys headed off, each going down a different aisle. Alex watched them go, proud of their willingness to step right up and do what he'd asked. He and Emily, each pushing a cart, went a different way. With no music playing in the background, the only sounds were occasional shouts as people argued, but for the most part, things seemed relatively calm.

They turned down the pasta aisle first. There wasn't a lot on the shelves, but they managed to grab several packages of spaghetti noodles, two boxes of rotini, three jars of spaghetti sauce, and the last two cases of ramen. He grabbed other items as he saw them and Emily did the same. Other shoppers came down the aisle, a frantic look in their eyes, which made his chest tighten with stress of his own. What would his family do when the food they had ran out? Not wanting to think that far ahead—they were probably in better shape than many other families—he focused on his task.

The fifteen minutes flew by, and after he and Emily had gone up and down several aisles, including the toiletries section, they pushed their full carts to the front of the store. A few moments later the boys joined him. Their carts were full too, much to Alex's relief.

"Great job," he said with a grin. Then the four of them got in one of the three long lines that had formed.

Since there was no need to put items on the non-working conveyor belt, the line moved pretty fast. Before long it was their turn.

"We have four carts," Alex said as he peeled off twelve hundred dollars, which seemed like highway robbery for what they'd gotten. But since that cash would soon only be useful as toilet paper, he didn't really care. The important thing was that they would have food.

He handed the clerk the money.

"You can bag it if you want to," she said. "Just take some bags and do it out of the way."

Deciding that might not be a bad idea, Alex grabbed a bunch of plastic bags from the turnstile and pushed his cart past the counter and over near the wall. The kids followed.

"Bag up what you can," he said to the kids as he handed out bags.

They quickly put their purchases in bags, then, pushing their filled carts, made their way toward the exit.

"Don't take the carts beyond the parking lot," the employee manning the door said as they reached the exit.

"Sure thing," Alex said, walking right past him, his kids following close behind.

Once they'd cleared the exit and started crossing the parking lot, Steven quietly said, "Are we really going to carry all of this stuff home?"

There was no way the four of them could carry everything.

"No," Alex said as he kept a brisk pace. "We'll combine what we can into two or three carts, but we're going to have to take the carts home."

"But that guy said not to."

Steven had always been a rule follower, which was a great thing—in normal times. These, however, were not normal times.

"It's okay," Jason said with a glance at Alex. "We can bring the carts back."

"Yeah," Alex said, although that certainly wasn't a priority.

"Okay," Steven said, his voice uncertain.

"It's more important that we get the food we need," Alex added.

When they were nearly to the street, they transferred all of the bags from one of the carts to the other three carts, but there was no way to combine further. Leaving that one cart in the parking lot, they pushed the other three out of the parking lot and began the trek home.

"Maybe Mom will be home when we get there," Emily said, her voice tinged with hope.

"Maybe so," Alex said. "Let's hurry home and find out."

CHAPTER 11

Melissa

MAKING SLOW BUT STEADY PROGRESS, Melissa and her group had nearly covered another three miles. John seemed to be having the most trouble, panting a bit as he struggled to keep up. But he was keeping up. Melissa felt bad for him. She was in decent shape and she was getting tired. Still, she pushed on, eager to get home, her mind on Alex and the kids. Was Alex walking too? Were the kids safe at home? What she wouldn't give for a way to reach out to them. For so long she'd taken modern technology for granted, the ability to text or call someone on a whim. Now though? Now, there was no way to communicate.

"What's that?" Dillon asked, his tone broadcasting shock as he pointed at something in the gutter in front of the Arctic Circle hamburger joint across the street from them.

The road was cluttered with stalled cars, but Melissa could

still see what he was pointing to. "Is that...," she began, squinting in the direction Dillon indicated, her hand shading her eyes from the sun, "a body?"

"Yeah," Rob said, "I think it is."

Her hand dropped to her side as her mouth fell open. The idea that a body would be lying out in the open stunned her. She'd never seen a dead body before. Wait. Was the person dead or just injured? "We should see if they need help," she said.

Rob frowned at her. "I think they're past help."

"How do you know? I mean, what if they're just hurt?"

He sighed. "And if they are? What are we supposed to do about it?"

He had a point there. Still. What if Alex was hurt? Or one of her kids? She hoped someone would help them.

"I'm going to check," she said as she stepped off of the sidewalk and into the street. Swerving around the first dead car, she heard Tamara call out, "Wait, I'm coming with you." Pausing, Melissa waited for Tamara to catch up. Then, to her surprise, all five men in their group began following.

As the group cleared all of the cars and the view of the body became clearer, Melissa began to regret her insistence to check on the person. It looked like a man. And she could see a puddle of blood under his head filling the gutter. A neat hole was centered in his forehead.

Yeah, it was doubtful he was still breathing.

Still, when she reached him, she knelt beside him and pressed two fingers to his neck in search of a pulse.

"Anything?" John asked from behind her.

She shook her head, then tilted her head up to him with a frown. "No. He's gone." She stood and faced their group, her stomach churning. Not only was she standing beside a dead body, but she'd actually *touched* it.

John's eyes went to the Arctic Circle behind her before widening as the blood drained from his face. "Get down," he shouted, shoving her to the ground as he pulled a handgun out of his waist holster.

Confused and terrified, Melissa flattened herself to the pavement. Half a second later several gunshots blasted around her. A chip of pavement hit her in the arm as a bullet struck the ground beside her. Screaming in surprise, she scrambled away, getting behind the nearest vehicle, a silver SUV. Frozen with fear, she curled up on the cold pavement for several long minutes, her eyes squeezed closed, but when she realized the shooting had stopped, she gathered her courage and maneuvered until she was able to peer underneath the SUV in the direction of her friends. To her horror, she saw three people down and bleeding. She couldn't tell who they were, although Tamara wasn't among them.

Frantic to know what was happening, she crawled to the front of the car before poking her head around the grill. First, she studied the area near the Arctic Circle, then she turned her gaze to the interior of the restaurant where she saw movement through the glass windows. At least two men were inside along with a woman. Wait! Was that ... Tamara? Tamara! What was she doing in there?

Closing her eyes in disbelief as to what this world was rapidly turning into, Melissa immediately realized that the shooters had taken Tamara.

"Is everyone okay?" she called out from her place of relative safety, although she knew the answer was no. Even so, she wanted to find out who was all right.

"I'm fine," John said, "but Rob, he's..." John's voice cracked. "He's dead."

Melissa's heart rattled at the news. "What?!" How could that be? He had been alive mere moments before. Breathing rapidly, she forced her emotions aside and forced herself to *think*. "What about everyone else? Is everyone else okay?" Although she already knew Tamara was definitely not.

"Dillon and Curtis were hit," John said.

She squeezed her eyes shut. "What about Tyler?" Melissa thought about how he'd come to her rescue at the shoe store, taking down that man who had been about to hit her.

"I'm okay," Tyler said, although his voice sounded strained.

Relieved, she softly exhaled and opened her eyes.

Scared to go where she would be exposed, Melissa also couldn't fathom staying where she was when her friends needed help. Gathering her courage, she scurried along the side of the car, still out of sight of the bad guys, until she reached the back end, then she moved toward the other side where she would be visible to all. On the lookout for the men who had attacked them—unprovoked!—she let her gaze ricochet between the interior of Arctic Circle and the outside area.

When she reached her friends, she took in the scene. Just like John had said, Rob was clearly dead. Dillon was bleeding profusely from his chest as well as his right shoulder and leg. He was unconscious and Melissa strained to see if his chest was moving. It didn't really seem like it. Tyler had his hands pressed against Curtis's stomach, but it didn't seem to be doing much to slow the blood flowing out. John moved toward Dillon, his hands hovering over Dillon's chest like he was unsure what to do, or if doing anything would even help.

"Is he alive?" Melissa asked, her voice tremulous.

John shook his head. "I don't know." He pressed his fingers against Dillon's throat, waited several moments, then tried another spot, then another. Finally, he turned to Melissa with tight eyes. "He's gone."

Shocked by the whole situation, Melissa felt the blood drain from her face. Then she remembered what she'd seen through the glass and felt her body go cold. "They took Tamara."

John nodded. "I know."

CHAPTER 12
Alex

Walking up the incline on 1300 East on their way home, it was a bit of work to push the shopping carts. Although with four of them and three carts, they were able to take turns. They moved forward in a single file, with Steven in front, Jason next, and Alex taking up the rear with Emily walking beside him.

The sound of a loud diesel engine climbing the hill grabbed their attention and they all slowed as they turned to watch an old pick-up truck coming their way. As it drew closer, Alex could see a man behind the wheel. He was alone. The man swerved around a stalled vehicle in the right lane, but instead of going back into his lane, he angled his truck toward them, crossing the double yellow line into the far-left lane. No one else was around on this stretch of road.

Heart rate picking up, Alex murmured, "Take the cart, Emily. And everyone keep walking."

She did as he asked and the four of them kept going, although they gave the truck side glances.

Alex slid his hand to his gun but didn't draw it, while at the same time putting himself between Emily and the truck that was now just behind them, almost hitting the curb. He wanted to put himself between the man and all three of his children, but with the way they were strung out along the sidewalk, that was impossible. Alex was proud to see Jason speed up so that he stood between Steven and the road.

Extremely uncomfortable with the entire situation, Alex decided it would be better to confront the man rather than turn his back on him. For all he knew, the man would shoot him in the back.

Stopping to face the man, who had his window down, Alex took in his long, scruffy beard and greasy hair, then said, "Can I help you with something?"

The man grinned, revealing teeth that looked like they were long overdue for a dental visit. "You got quite a haul there."

"What's it to you?"

He raised his hands like he meant no harm. "Just stating a fact."

"Like I said, what's it to you?"

He lowered his hands out of sight, which put Alex on alert. He had no idea if the man had a gun sitting on his lap.

"Looks like there's enough to share," the man said.

"There's not," Alex shot back.

The man began to softly chuckle, then the volume increased until he threw his head back with laughter. Two seconds later the sound cut off abruptly and he narrowed his eyes at Alex. "What if I say there is?"

Okay. Alex had had enough. For the third time that day he withdrew his gun. Cupping his right hand with his left, he aimed at the man's head. "There's not. Now move along." He heard Emily gasp, but he ignored her. Hating that his children had to witness this, he was realistic enough to know that it was something they would have to get used to. Desperately hoping that the sight of the gun would end the situation, Alex felt adrenaline flooding his veins.

But what if it doesn't? he asked himself. Would he be willing to actually shoot—to kill—another human? Especially in front of his children?

Praying that wouldn't be necessary, he waited to see what the man would do.

Without warning, the man lifted a handgun and pointed it at Jason, who was the largest target of Alex's three children. "Looks like we have a standoff," he said, wearing a menacing grin. "And wouldn't you know? Not a cop to be found." He chuckled. "Society's in the crapper now, which means I can do what I want." Narrowing his eyes at Alex, he said, "Drop your weapon and then load all that stuff into my truck and maybe I won't shoot your kid."

Alex knew he should have taken the shot the moment the man's hands had started to come up, but he was an engineer, not a soldier. He didn't have the training or the muscle memory to be that fast.

But that didn't mean he had to stand down now.

"Okay," he said, as if he was about to comply. He lowered his gun fractionally, his gaze glued to the man's hands. The man must have believed Alex was giving in, because Alex could see the man's gun lower, just a bit. Which is when Alex retook his aim and pulled the trigger. The man jerked back, hit in the shoulder. Not waiting to see if he was going to shoot back, Alex stepped closer while taking another shot and another, until the threat had been neutralized.

Emily was screaming, but Alex tuned her out, his eyes intensely focused on the man in the truck, who was slumped forward, his head resting on the steering wheel, blood everywhere. With his gun still pointed at the man, Alex moved to the open window where he reached inside and pressed two fingers against his neck. Pausing, he felt for a pulse, but there was none. Which is when it hit him—he'd killed a man.

He was going to shoot Jason, his inner voice reminded him.

True though that was, he still began to feel a slight out of body experience that he recognized as shock.

He lifted the man's handgun from where the man had dropped it in his lap, then he tucked his Glock back in his waist holster and the man's gun into the back of his jeans.

Alex realized the truck's motor had shut off. Thinking it was somehow from the EMP, when he peered inside and saw that the truck had a manual transmission, he realized the man's foot had simply slipped off of the clutch, stalling the engine.

"Dad!" Jason said as he came up beside him. "Dad! Are you okay?"

Slowly turning to face his son—the son who could have been killed instead of the man in the truck—Alex dragged in a sharp breath, then focused on Jason before turning to Steven, whose mouth was hanging open, then Emily, who was sobbing.

"I'm okay," Alex said. "We're all okay."

"Is he...," Jason began, his eyes going between Alex and the man, "is he dead?"

Nodding, Alex said, "Yeah."

Jason seemed to relax at that. "Do you think he would have shot me?"

Alex shook his head. "I don't know. But I...I couldn't take that chance."

A small smile curved Jason's lips. "I should hope not, Dad."

Eyebrows bunching, Alex gazed at his oldest child. "Doesn't it bother you that I...*killed* him?"

Jason chewed on his lower lip. "Is it bad that it doesn't? I mean, you *had* to." He paused. "Even if you'd let him take our stuff, what if he'd..." he glanced at his sister, who was beginning to calm down. Jason's voice went to a whisper. "What if he'd taken Emily too?"

That hadn't even occurred to Alex, and there was no way to know if the man would have stooped that low. But Jason was right. There would have been nothing Alex could have done to stop him.

Yes. Putting him down had been the only thing he could have done to protect his family.

Slowly nodding, Alex let a grim smile lift his lips. "You're right, Jason. Thank you."

Stepping away from the truck, Alex went to Emily and pulled her into his arms. She lay her head against his shoulder as small, shuddering breaths left her. "It's okay, sweetheart," he murmured. He held her until she drew away.

"Thank you for taking care of us, Dad," she said, her face tear-streaked.

Putting both hands on her shoulders, he locked eyes with her. "Of course. I will do whatever I have to do to protect you guys."

CHAPTER 13

Alex

"Dad?" Steven said from beside him.

Alex turned to face him. "Yeah, buddy?"

"I think..." he looked down, then lifted his eyes to Alex's. "I think we all need to carry a gun."

Alex recoiled at the thought. His thirteen-year-old carrying? That was absurd, right?

"Steven's right," Jason said. "What if that guy had shot you, Dad? We'd all be sitting ducks."

Swiveling his head to Jason, Alex was flummoxed. Because his son—both sons—were right. As much as he loathed the idea—and for heaven's sake, it was only day one—they needed more than just him for defense.

His thoughts whirled—how dangerous would it be to arm his children? What would Melissa say? Where was Melissa? Shaking his head, he closed his eyes. He couldn't get distracted by what he had no control over. "Let me think about it, okay?"

Both boys nodded.

"If they're going to have guns," Emily said, "then I should have one too."

He held up his hands in surrender. "Right now we need to get home, all right?"

"Uh, Dad?" Jason said.

"Yeah?"

He glanced at the truck. "I don't think that guy needs his truck anymore. Maybe we should, you know, take it."

Alex's immediate reaction was to say no. It would feel like he'd killed a man for his vehicle, which logically he knew wasn't the case at all. Still, that's how it felt.

"We can find Mom!" Steven said, his voice filled with possibility.

That got Alex's attention, which was when he realized that it would be foolish to pass up the opportunity to acquire one of the rare vehicles that ran. Still, he had to make it clear to his kids that this situation wasn't optimal.

"For the record," he began, "I wish that man had never stopped. I hate that I had to kill him. But..." he frowned and shook his head as he sighed and looked at the ground. "But," he began again, his voice softer, "if this truck can help us find Mom, then I say yes. We should take it."

Nodding with a soberness that surprised Alex, Jason said, "Good call, Dad."

"All right," Alex said. "You guys load the bed with the stuff from the shopping carts and I'll, uh, I'll remove the man from the cab."

They immediately got to work transferring all the bags from the carts to the bed of the truck while Alex went to the driver's door and pulled it open. The man was right where he'd been since Alex had shot him. Softly sighing, Alex grabbed the man's left arm and began tugging. Moments later the man fell out of the truck and onto the pavement.

"Here, Dad," Jason said, "let me help."

Proud of his son for stepping up, Alex worked with Jason to lift the man from the pavement and set him on the grass under one of the trees that lined the sidewalk.

"Are we just gonna leave him here?" Jason asked, his voice soft.

Though it might seem disrespectful to not take the time to bury the man, Alex had more pressing things to do, so he nodded. "Yeah. We need to find Mom. I mean, it'll be dark soon and she's still out there."

Jason nodded. "I agree."

Somehow, hearing that helped assuage Alex's guilt at leaving the man.

"We're done," Emily said a few moments later.

Alex stepped between her and the body. She didn't need to see it up close and personal. "Great. Hop in the passenger side. You boys get in the bed of the truck."

While they did that, Alex stared at the blood smeared on the driver's side seat, then clenched his jaw before climbing inside. After pushing in the clutch, Alex started the engine back up, and after a short drive, they pulled into their driveway.

The boys hopped out of the bed of the truck.

"Do you know how to manually open the garage door?" Alex asked Jason.

"That red string on the inside, right?"

"Yeah."

"Then yeah. Hold on a sec."

When the garage door slid open from the inside a few minutes later, Alex pulled the truck into the garage. With the four of them helping, it didn't take long to get the food they'd purchased moved into the kitchen.

"We'll sort through it later," Alex said, then with a grim smile, he added, "I'll be back in a minute." Taking the stairs two at a time, he reached the top, then turned right to go into the master bedroom. Once there, he took the dead man's gun from the back of his jeans. He dropped the magazine and confirmed it was loaded, then, after examining the gun further, he reinserted the magazine before going to his gun safe. He found the key he'd hidden earlier and opened the safe.

First, he put the dead man's gun on a shelf. Next, he removed his AR-15 and carried it into the bedroom where light from the window flooded the room. After a brief examination of the black rifle, he set it on his bed then went back to his safe and grabbed extra magazines for both the AR and the Glock 19. He also removed a .40 caliber pistol for Jason and a spare holster, as well as a tactical knife and sheath, then he locked the safe and put the key back.

Dumping out the backpack he'd tossed on the bed earlier, he kept the first-aid kit, snacks, and water, and added the spare mags, then he attached the horizontal knife sheath to his belt at his back and inserted the knife. Going back into his closet, he grabbed a hoodie and tugged it over his head, pulling it down to cover the knife. He zipped the backpack closed, tossed it over one shoulder and the AR over the other, then picked up the .40 and the spare holster and headed back downstairs.

Walking into the kitchen, he set the .40 and the spare holster on the counter and announced, "We should bring extra water and snacks." If all of them were going, what he had in his pack wouldn't be enough.

All three kids nodded and began gathering what they needed. As they dug through the pantry, Alex went to the junk drawer. He was pretty sure there was an old map of Salt Lake City and the outlying cities in there. Once they'd started relying on the GPS on their phones, the paper maps had been tossed, but for some reason he'd kept one copy around. It took him a minute to find it, but once he did, he opened it up and spread it out on the table, using his finger to trace the routes he would search.

Realizing how intense this search would be, he had second thoughts about bringing the kids. They would be safer at home, right?

He straightened to find them organizing water bottles and

snacks.

With a mixture of guilt and relief, he said, "Guys?" They all looked his way, their faces filled with expectation. Clearing his throat, he said, "I've decided to go look for Mom by myself."

"No, Dad," Jason said with a strong shake of his head. "No way. I'm going with you."

"Me too," Steven said, although with the way his eyebrows had gone up, it felt more like a question than a statement.

Playing through several possible scenarios of what could happen, Alex considered the best course of action. Then he came to a decision. "Okay. Here's what we're going to do. Steven, you and Emily are going to stay here and hold down the fort. Jason, you're coming with me."

A broad smile burst upon Jason's lips, but Steven's shoulders sagged. Emily, however, let out a huge breath like she was relieved.

"That's not fair, Dad," Steven said. "I want to come too."

Alex strode across the room to where Steven was holding a box of granola bars and offered him a steady gaze. "I need you here, son." His voice was low but confident. He glanced at Emily before meeting Steven's disappointed eyes. "I don't want to take your sister out there and I don't want to leave her on her own. I need you to protect her."

Steven seemed to consider this before huffing out a sigh, then he nodded. "All right. Fine."

"Thanks, Steven." Then Alex placed his hands on Steven's shoulders. "I'm counting on you."

At Alex's sober words, anxiety tightened Steven's eyes. "What should I do if..." he shook his head like he didn't want to consider the possibilities.

"If you feel like you're in danger," Alex said, "go next door to Stan's house."

"Okay."

"But I think you'll be perfectly fine here," he added. "If someone comes to the door, don't answer, okay? Unless it's Mom." He could only hope she got home while he was gone.

"Okay, Dad."

Alex gave first Steven, then Emily, a hug, then he went to the counter and picked up the pistol and the holster before turning to Jason and holding them out to him. He hated that he had to arm his teenaged son, but leaving him defenseless wasn't an option. Besides, they'd spent a decent amount of time at the firing range. Jason had the skill and knowledge he needed to handle a firearm.

Jason took the gun, his eyes kind of wide.

"You can use this to carry it," Alex said, handing him an inside-the-waistband holster.

Jason nodded. He set the gun on the table, put on the holster, then tucked the gun away.

"What about me?" Steven asked, his eyes filled with a mix of hope and uncertainty.

"For now," Alex said, "Jason is the only one who will be armed. He has more experience handling a gun. You and Emily need more training before I hand a gun over to either one of you." Heaven forbid *that* should ever be necessary.

Steven nodded, his expression serious like he understood. "Okay."

After folding the map and tucking it under his arm, Alex nodded toward Jason. "Let's go."

A short time later they were backing out of the garage. When they'd cleared the door, Steven gave them a wave before pulling it closed. Alex waved back, his heart in his throat at leaving his two younger children alone. Not wanting to voice his fears, Alex glanced at Jason, who said exactly what was on Alex's mind.

"Do you think they'll be okay, Dad?"

"They'll be safer staying in our house than out here with us." And really, he believed that was true. As much as he hated leaving them on their own, at least being at home was a more controlled environment and out of danger.

Shifting his attention to the task at hand, he left the neighborhood before turning left on 1300 East, heading north. "I have no idea where Mom is, so we'll try several different routes and pray we find her."

"How much fuel do we have?"

Alex checked the gauge. "Looks like about half a tank." He glanced at Jason. "Should be enough for a while."

Jason nodded. "Okay."

Driving slowly—to keep an eye out for Melissa, but also because of the all the stalled cars he had to dodge—Alex worried that in the hour of remaining daylight they wouldn't get very far. And then finding her would become very difficult indeed.

CHAPTER 14

Melissa

"WHAT ARE WE GOING TO DO?" Melissa asked. "I mean, we can't leave Tamara in there. With them." Not wanting to consider why the men had taken her friend, when Melissa recognized that it could just as easily have been her, she knew they had to do whatever they could to rescue Tamara.

"He's dead," Tyler shouted as he leaned back on his heels in front of Curtis. He turned and stared at Melissa and John, his mouth hanging open as he rubbed his eyebrow. He blinked several times. "They killed him."

Terrified that the men inside were going to open fire again, Melissa's gaze flicked to the Arctic Circle, but she didn't see anyone. She began moving behind the SUV again. "We need to get out of sight."

John nodded before he crawled in her direction, but then he stopped and looked at Tyler, who seemed to be in shock.

"Tyler," John said, his tone urgent. "Tyler, come on. We need to move."

Tyler just looked at him like he didn't understand what was happening. John grabbed Tyler's arm and gave him a yank. "Let's go."

Tyler seemed to come out of his stupor, nodding as he sighed, then he followed.

Once all three of them were safely out of the range of the shooters, Melissa looked at the men with her. Their group had shrunk from seven to three. But it would grow to four once they got Tamara back. She would make sure of it. Somehow. Even so, they'd lost three people. No, not lost. Her friends had been murdered. In cold blood. For no reason. Well, yes, she knew the reason. Those men had wanted to take Tamara.

The thought of her friend, who was barely thirty, being taken by those thugs made Melissa sick.

"We have to get Tamara," Melissa said, her eyes going between Tyler and John.

John nodded like he'd been thinking the same thing.

"But how?" Tyler asked. "The men who took her..." he shook his head, his eyes tightening. "They're cold-blooded killers."

Heart thudding painfully in her chest, Melissa nodded. "Which is exactly why we need to get Tamara back. Before they hurt her. Or worse."

"Any idea how?" John asked.

Melissa had never been into war-gaming or anything like it, but she was a problem solver. Or at least a project manager, which was basically the same thing. *I'll look at this like a project,* she thought. That was the only way to feel like she wasn't drowning. Because if she thought about the stakes—Tamara's life—she didn't know if she would be able to remain levelheaded.

Briefly closing her eyes, she tried to picture the area around the Arctic Circle but she couldn't remember exactly what she'd seen. So, she peered around the front of the SUV and let her gaze wander. Which is when she came up with a plan of sorts.

Fully behind the SUV again, she looked between Tyler and John. "We can use the cars here and in the parking lot to get close to the building without them seeing us. We'll have to be stealthy, but we can do it, right?" She desperately hoped they would approve of her plan, because she had no other ideas.

"What do we do once we get to the building?" John asked. "I mean, we have no idea where they are or how many there are."

Suppressing a sigh, Melissa frowned. Although he'd brought up a valid concern, at least he hadn't shot down her idea. "Right."

"Doesn't matter," Tyler said, his jaw set. "We can't leave your friend in there."

Grateful that he was willing to give it a try, Melissa nodded. Then she thought of a new problem. "You both have guns, but I..." she grimaced as she held up her empty hands and shook her head. "Any ideas on what I can use as a weapon?"

All three of them looked around.

"Wait," John said. "Didn't Dillon have a knife?"

"Yeah," Tyler said. "He did."

Melissa recalled the conversation outside the shoe store when they'd discussed who had a weapon and Dillon showing them his knife. A rather small knife. The saying *Don't bring a knife to a gun fight* rang through her head. True as that was, a knife was better than nothing. "That'll have to do." Without waiting for anyone to volunteer, Melissa began making her way back to the front of the SUV, which was closest to Dillon.

"Where are you going?" John asked, his voice just above a whisper.

Not bothering to look back, she said, "To get the knife." Then she slid past the SUV's grill. She could hear John calling her back, but she was committed now. Besides, she could do it a lot faster than he could, she was sure. And Tyler still seemed to be struggling with his friend dying. She was struggling too, but she'd locked those feelings into a mental box where she would deal with them later. For now, she had to focus on what was happening, focus on what she had to do.

After a long look at the Arctic Circle to make sure no one was about to shoot her, she scrambled over to Dillon. He was young, only in his twenties, and now his life was over.

Reminding herself to put her grief aside, she concentrated on digging through his pockets until she found the knife he'd shown them. Just as she remembered, it wasn't very big, but it would have to do.

Moments later she was back on the safe side of the SUV.

"You didn't have to do that," John said. "Tyler or I could have gotten it."

Grinning, she held the knife up like a trophy. "Yeah? Well, I got it."

John smiled in return.

Tyler seemed more subdued. "They could have taken you too."

The thought had crossed her mind. What if she'd come around the SUV only to find a gun pointed at her head and the men ready to drag her away? Shoving aside that imagery, she said, "But they didn't."

"Okay," Tyler said, obviously ready to move on. "Once we get to that building, we'll have to find a door that's unlocked. And then we'll have to go in and surprise them."

None of them asked what they would do if the door was locked.

Melissa looked around and saw a few people walking along the sidewalk on the other side of the road, evidently just arriving and oblivious to the gun battle that had recently taken place. Then she saw a pair of men pointing toward the bodies of her dead friends before looking at her, John, and Tyler hunkered down behind the SUV.

The men hurried on their way, apparently not wanting any part of the trouble that was brewing.

She couldn't blame them, but it would be nice to have some help. But no help was coming. She knew that. It was just hard to accept. But it was the world she lived in now. The world they *all* lived in.

"There aren't enough cars to conceal us all the way to the building," Tyler said as he poked his head around the SUV.

That was true and Melissa worried what would happen if the bad guys saw them approaching. Nothing good, she was sure of that. Then she turned and looked to the west. The sun would be going down in an hour or so. Should they wait for that? What if Tamara was dead by then? But what good would it do anyone if they were shot before they ever had the chance to get close? What would happen to her children if she was dead? Because she had no idea where Alex was. Most likely he was still on his way home, which meant her children were by themselves. She had to make it out of this alive and then get home to her family.

CHAPTER 15

Melissa

"We should wait until dark to go after Tamara." Melissa hated admitting that, but she didn't see any other option.

Tyler frowned, then nodded. "I agree."

John nodded as well. "I think that's the smart move."

Glad they were all on the same page, Melissa removed her backpack purse from her shoulders, then took out a protein bar before leaning against the SUV's rear tire. When she noticed John and Tyler watching her, she raised her eyebrows. "Do you guys want one?"

"That would be great," Tyler said.

"I'm good," John said as he took his pack off of his back and pulled out a granola bar.

She handed a protein bar to Tyler, noticing that she only had two left. But sharing was important because they would need their energy if they were to have a chance to succeed in rescuing Tamara.

John took a bottle of water out of his pack and held it up. "Water?"

Tyler nodded and John gave him the unopened bottle while Melissa shook her head. "I've got my own, but thanks."

Savoring every bite of her dark chocolate, peanut, and almond protein bar, Melissa mentally played out how Tamara's rescue could go, keeping it all positive even though she knew their chances of success were not all that high. Not knowing what else to do, she said a silent prayer asking for help—to succeed somehow, to figure out how to make it work, to perhaps even send someone to assist them, someone who would know what to do.

As the sun began its descent, Melissa felt a distinct chill in the air. She rubbed her arms in an attempt to warm up, but she knew it was supposed to get down to freezing that night. It was March in Salt Lake City, after all. Good thing she'd chosen to put her sweater on before leaving the office. If she hadn't, wearing only her long-sleeved shirt wouldn't have been enough.

Multiple people passed their position, although they were almost always on the sidewalk across the street, too far for conversation. Too far to care what was happening with Melissa and her group. One man, however, was walking right down the middle of the road. When he reached them, he paused, his eyes going from the three of them to the nearby bodies, then back to them.

"What happened here?" he asked, his forehead furrowed.

Melissa appraised him, taking in his neat haircut, clean jeans, and dark gray hoodie. Who was this guy and why was he stopping?

"We were attacked," Melissa said. "They took our friend."

The man's eyebrows shot up, then his gaze started bouncing from one place to another like he was searching for danger. Seconds later he squatted near them, his eyes still on the move. "Where are they now?"

"In the Arctic Circle," John said.

The man zeroed in on John. "Why are you still here? Are they..." he looked around again, "taking potshots at you?"

"No," John said, drawing the man's attention back to him. "They stopped shooting after they took Tamara a couple of hours ago."

The man slowly nodded. "You're going to try to rescue her." It wasn't a question.

Was this a trick? Was he one of the men who had taken Tamara, now posing as an innocent bystander so he could get more information? Wary, Melissa glanced at John, whose lips were flat, then at Tyler, whose eyes were narrowed at the man.

"Why do you want to know?" Tyler asked, and Melissa remembered that he'd said he was an attorney. She'd never asked him what he specialized in. Maybe he was a criminal attorney, which would probably give him a sixth sense of sorts to recognize those up to no good. And which was probably also the reason he carried a gun.

The man held his hands up in surrender. "Just asking."

Then his lips pressed into a thin line. "I was going to offer to help, but if you've got it under control, then I'll be on my way."

All of a sudden Melissa remembered her silent prayer asking for help, which included a plea for someone who had more experience and more knowledge. Someone who could actually make this work.

"What's your name?" she asked. Although she was eager for help, she was still going to be cautious.

He turned to her, looking directly in her eyes like he knew who he was and was proud of it. "Eric. Eric Barker."

Instantly, Melissa knew he was a good person. She could *feel* it. The warmth in her chest confirmed it. He could help them. She knew it.

A smile curved her lips. "I'm Melissa." She held out her hand. He took it, his grip firm and strong. When he released her hand, she glanced at John and Tyler. They were watching the exchange with interest. Melissa faced Eric again. "We could use your help."

"Hold on," Tyler said.

Melissa turned to him, not surprised that he was objecting. That had been her first instinct as well. Wanting to get Tyler and John on board, she shifted her attention to Eric. "Why do you think you can help?"

One side of Eric's mouth tilted up. "You could say I have some experience with hostage situations."

Melissa knew it. He *was* an answer to prayer. Trying not to become giddy with relief, Melissa nodded, her expression impassive.

"Care to elaborate?" Tyler asked.

"Not really," Eric replied.

"Are you SWAT?" John asked.

Eric turned to him, then shook his head. "Nope."

"Military," Tyler stated.

Eric's grin was back. "What's your plan?"

Melissa's guess was that he must be Special Ops. Good. They could use someone with training and experience. Slightly embarrassed about what they'd come up with, she grimaced. "We thought we'd use the cars as cover to get close to the building. After that?" She shrugged then looked at him with hope-filled eyes. "We're open to suggestions."

Slowly nodding, Eric's lips pursed, then he met each of their inquisitive eyes before saying, "Back soon." At that, he crept away, staying behind the nearby cars as he moved. He headed south, in the direction Melissa and her group had originally been going.

"What do you think he's doing?" John asked, rising on his knees to try to follow Eric's progress.

Melissa was watching too, but when he vanished from sight moments later, she turned to John and Tyler with a sigh. "I assume he's checking things out."

"Recon," Tyler said with a frown. "But what makes you think we can trust him? For all we know, he's going straight to the bad guys and...I don't know. Cut a deal or something."

"Why would he do that?" Melissa asked, horrified by the idea of the man she believed was there to help turning on them.

"In my experience," Tyler said with a scowl, "most people are only out to help themselves. And now, with society collapsing?" He shook his head. "It's only going to get worse."

"What kind of attorney are you?" Melissa asked.

"Criminal defense."

Just what she thought. "Not everyone is bad, Tyler."

He chuckled. "I know."

"But you've seen the worst of people."

He nodded. "Yeah. I have."

"Do you believe this guy will really help us?" John asked Melissa.

Considering the stakes, Melissa was surprised when she didn't even hesitate. "Yeah. I do."

"Why?" Tyler asked, his eyebrows bunching. "Why would he help a bunch of complete strangers?"

"I think he's Special Ops," Melissa said. "So, he's in the military. A lot of people join the military because they want to defeat the bad guys or want to help people or both." She lifted one shoulder in a shrug. "He's just doing what he was trained to do, what he wants to do." And he was an answer to a prayer.

"Okay, yeah," Tyler said. "I guess I can see that."

By the time Eric returned, his expression serious, the sun was sinking into the horizon. "All right," he said as he hunkered down beside them. "I scouted out the best approach and I've formulated a plan."

He sketched out what he had in mind. Melissa was glad he'd shown up. She never would have come up with anything remotely similar to what he had, although she knew that even with his help, success was not assured.

CHAPTER 16

Alex

ALEX AND JASON drove slowly north along 1300 East, their progress hampered by all the stalled cars. Fortunately, the EMP had hit in the mid-afternoon, so the road wasn't nearly as clogged with dead cars as it would have been if it had hit during commute time. Still, there were plenty that they had to circumvent.

With his AR-15 lying across his lap, his Glock on his hip, and Jason armed beside him, he felt somewhat prepared for what they might face. It helped that they were in a truck, a box of metal that surrounded them. Then he remembered how he'd gotten this means of transportation. He'd killed a man. Sure, he'd had a good reason, but it didn't make it any easier to accept. Now that things were quiet, at least for the moment, he couldn't help but reflect on how dark he felt after having taken a human life. He really hoped he wouldn't have to take another, although seeing as this was only day one of the apocalypse and what he'd already had to do, it seemed unlikely that he would never have to kill again.

Frowning deeply at the thought, he scanned every woman he saw walking along the street, some on the sidewalk and some in the road. None were Melissa. It was easy to get a close look, seeing as how he and Jason were only going about ten miles an hour. They'd only been on the road for thirty minutes, but Alex had to admit that he was already getting discouraged. It had been hours since the EMP had shattered their lives, and darkness would be descending soon. At the rate they were going, there was no way they would be able to cover all of Melissa's possible routes before dark. And it wasn't as if he could simply drive the route she normally took home. Like him, she usually drove the Interstate each day. But that was when she had a car. He seriously doubted she would have chosen to walk home along I-15. Most likely, as he had done, she would take surface streets. The question was, which ones? There were a number of options and he had no idea which she had chosen. If she was with a group—and he dearly hoped she was—then the most direct route might not have been an option. Not if others in her group needed to veer off from the route Melissa would want to take. She would most likely go where the group went rather than go off on her own. She might even be spending the night somewhere and not on the road at all.

Frustrated beyond reason, Alex clenched his jaw but kept moving. Forward, always forward.

"Wait!" Jason called out.

Alex slammed on the brakes, his heart racing as his gaze shot in the direction Jason was studying. There was a moderate-sized group walking on the sidewalk across the street, including several women. Squinting in their direction, Alex willed Melissa to be among them, but none of them looked like her.

"Nope, not her." Jason turned to Alex with a pained expression, his voice filled with dejection. "Sorry, Dad."

"That's okay." But inside, Alex's heart dropped with sharp disappointment.

"She's out there somewhere, so we'll find her." Jason's eyes tightened with worry. "We have to."

"We do and we will." Fresh determination at his son's words flowed through him as he accelerated and the truck lurched forward.

A while later, Jason said, "Have you noticed that there aren't as many people now as there were earlier?"

They'd seen plenty of people walking—many stopping to stare at them as they drove by, some trying to flag them down. But Jason was right. The numbers had thinned considerably. "Yeah, I did." Alex glanced to his left at the setting sun. "Guess they don't want to be outdoors once the sun goes down." Not only was it going to get cold, but the dangers after dark would multiply exponentially. The thought of Melissa having to deal with both of those things made his anxiety skyrocket.

Eventually they reached the intersection of 1300 East and

Van Winkle Expressway. Pausing like he was waiting for the light to turn green, Alex considered which way to go. They'd gone far enough north that it seemed unlikely that they would see Melissa on this route. It was time to try another path. But which way should they head? They had to find her!

Desperation sat like a stone in Alex's gut.

"Let me see the map," Alex said as he put the truck in neutral and let the clutch out. Jason handed it over and Alex unfolded it before laying it across the steering wheel. "We're here," he said, tapping the intersection where they sat. "Mom started off here." Feeling completely blind as to her location, he chewed on his lip as he considered the roads she might have taken. "She could have gone this way," he said, tracing his finger along one route. "Or this way." He paused. "Or *this* way. And who knows how far she's gotten. Is she north of us or has she made it farther south?"

About to wad up the map and toss it out the window in frustration, instead he drew in several steadying breaths, then closed his eyes and thought about Melissa—her selfless nature, the way she was always there for him and their children, how hard she worked. He loved her so much. If anything happened to her, he didn't know if he would be able to deal with it.

He had to calm down, had to listen to his gut.

Opening his eyes, he pushed in the clutch, shifted into first, then slowly let the clutch out as he gently accelerated. The truck moved forward until it was nearly in the center of the intersection, although with several non-working cars blocking the way, he had to stop before he got that far. Putting the truck back in neutral, he looked to the left, northwest on Van Winkle. At a minimum, he had to go that way. Then he would need to decide whether to take 900 East, the same road he'd traversed earlier, or continue along Van Winkle until it turned into 700 East. And if he chose 900 East, he would have to decide whether to go north or south.

Feeling overwhelmed, he turned to Jason as if his seventeen-year-old son would have the answer. "What do you think?"

His lips pursing, he shook his head and shrugged. "Beats me."

Nodding in agreement, Alex handed Jason the map, then put the truck in gear and moved forward, angling left onto Van Winkle Expressway. It was strange how he didn't have to wait for a light to turn green or for a break in traffic before he could cross all of those lanes.

Carefully swerving around the inoperative cars, he steered the truck onward. It didn't take long to reach 900 East where he drew to a stop.

The sun had nearly set, but Alex was nowhere near ready to give up. Melissa was close. She had to be. With the truck idling and sitting in the middle of the intersection, Alex looked to his right—north on 900 East, then to his left—south on that same road—and finally studied the road straight ahead. Three options. One which may actually lead to his wife. The others would lead to wasted time and even potentially, danger.

He and Jason had been fortunate in the hour since they'd left home. No one had attacked them. Of course, it helped that they were in a vehicle and were minding their own business. Still, he was grateful.

Estimating that it had been over four hours since the EMP had drastically changed life as they knew it, he tried to guess how far Melissa might have gone had she come this way. Her office was approximately eight miles north, so it was possible she'd passed by here already and was well on her way home. Even so, something tugged at him to continue along Van Winkle, which turned into 700 East. It made no sense, really. Unless she'd run into trouble. That would slow her down. Way down.

What if she was hurt? He thought about the woman on the bike, Cassie. She'd injured her ankle and had needed his help to get home. It had been slow going with her bum ankle. What if something like that had happened to Melissa?

Not wanting to consider all that could have gone wrong, and despite logic telling him to turn south on 900 East, he went with his gut, which told him to go straight.

Feeling good now that a decision had been made, he drove forward.

As they slowly drove, Alex noted the concrete barriers lining both sides of the Expressway, and just on the other side of the barriers were higher fences lending privacy to backyards. A wide, grassy median divided the two directions of roadway and there was no shoulder on this part of the Expressway.

They approached a curve, one he couldn't see beyond. Expecting their passage to be the same as they'd experienced so far, when they came around the bend and saw a pile-up of cars that looked like it had been caused by a chain-reaction, he had no choice but to stop.

"Any way around?" Jason asked, his forehead furrowed.

Alex wondered the same thing. People drove fast on this Expressway. When the EMP had hit and cars had shut off abruptly, taking away power steering and power breaks, mayhem had clearly ensued. So much so that even the grassy median was blocked. Drivers must have swerved into the median to avoid crashing into other cars.

There was no way around.

"Maybe we should go back," Jason suggested.

Alex considered it and it seemed the logical thing to do, but something told him to keep going.

Wearing a grim expression, he turned to Jason. "We go on foot."

CHAPTER 17

Melissa

DARKNESS HAD FALLEN, which meant it was time to put Eric's plan into motion.

"Are you sure you're up to this?" Eric asked Melissa as they went over the plan one last time.

When he'd first told her what he had in mind and her role in it, her initial reaction had been to say he needed to come up with something else, but the more she thought about it, the more it made sense.

Terrified as she was, she nodded. She had to do this. For Tamara. "Yeah."

"Don't forget your backpack," Eric said to John, then the four of them set off into the dark, heading the same way Eric had gone earlier when he'd been on his reconnaissance mission. Using the stalled cars as cover, they crept down the street, and when they reached the far end of the neighboring building, a large three-story, they stood and trotted to the front corner, pausing to fill John's backpack with decorative rocks from the landscaping before making their way to the back side of the building and finally backtracking toward the parking lot that was adjacent to the Arctic Circle. They'd made a giant U, starting from where they'd been hiding earlier and ending in the parking lot south of their target. The lot was full of cars and no people were in that area.

The four of them ducked behind a car, which was when Eric pointed to a side door on the Arctic Circle. There were no windows on that side of the building. They all nodded in understanding. Then he pointed to John and motioned to the place he wanted him to go, then he did the same with Tyler. The men split off, going in opposite directions but to places that had a clear line of sight to the building door.

Next, Eric raised his eyebrows at Melissa. Heart slamming in her chest with a fear she'd never known before, she drew in a deep breath, exhaled, then nodded.

With a single nod, Eric stood and dashed over to the door, the heavy backpack in his hands. He dropped it to the left of the door before moving to the right of it, then pressed his back against the wall. When he was in place, Melissa got to her feet and came out from behind the car before beginning to stumble in the direction of the door. She was supposed to act injured, but her nervousness made it easy to walk unsteadily.

"Hello?" she called out. "Is anyone in there? I need help."

Her eyes went to Eric, who was watching her closely. Then

a terrifying thought leapt into her mind. What if this was all a trap? A way to get her inside with the bad guys? What if Eric was with them? Then out of her peripheral vision she saw John and Tyler, guns trained in their direction, not thirty feet away. If this was a trap, then Eric was taking a big chance of getting shot by her friends.

No, she told herself. *Eric is legit. He's really here to help.*

Still, her heart slammed harder.

"Hello?" she called out again moments before reaching the door. Eric gave her a single nod. She was at the door. Pounding on it, Melissa shouted, "Hello? Is anyone there?"

A moment later, the knob began to turn. Beyond terrified that this was going to go all wrong and she would shift from rescuer to victim, she held steady.

"Let me in!" she shouted, her voice shaking with fear. "Please!"

The door cracked open, swinging outward. It was pitch black inside the building, but the light from the moon slightly illuminated the face of a man peering out, the gun in his hand pointed right at Melissa. She peed her pants a little, but amazed herself that she stayed in place rather than turning around and running for her life. Okay, maybe the fear-paralysis had something to do with it.

"You alone?" the man asked, his voice gravel-rough, his face nearly covered in tattoos.

Using all her self-control to keep her eyes on him rather than flicking in Eric's direction, Melissa nodded. "Can you help me?"

The man looked her up and down, which sent a shiver of revulsion through her, then he grinned, which made her want to vomit.

He lowered his gun and stepped forward, pushing the door open wider.

"Thank you," she managed to squeak out. Then she looked to her left before lifting her gaze to his face. "Can you help me carry my bag in? It's really heavy." Because it was mostly full of rocks.

The man's gaze went to the bulging backpack. "Whatcha got in there?"

"Food, mostly," Melissa said with a look she hoped conveyed that she didn't know how valuable food was.

"Any weapons?"

"My brother's gun, but I don't know how to use it."

The man's eyebrows shot up and the glint in his eye told Melissa that Eric's assumptions had been good.

"Sure," he said, his eyes never leaving the bag. "I can get it for you."

She forced a bright smile onto her lips. "Thank you so much."

The man's eyes snapped to her but then went right back to the bag. "Hold the door open for me."

This wasn't part of the plan. Resisting the almost overpowering urge to look where Eric was poised and waiting to the right of the door, Melissa swallowed her fear at being so close to the inside of the building, but it was hard to get down. Then she nodded and stepped forward before putting her hand against the door to keep the automatic hinge from doing its job and closing the door, which would lock them out.

To her amazement, the man stepped out of the building, never looking in the direction Eric stood, and bent toward the backpack. The moment his hand clasped the strap, Eric leapt into view and plunged a knife into the man's neck, twisting it vigorously. Blood gushed out as the man collapsed to the ground.

Rather shocked at the violence, when Melissa recalled the way this man and his buddies had murdered three of her friends and taken Tamara without a second thought, any sadness she may have felt evaporated.

"Hey," a deep voice called out from inside. "Bruce. What's going on out there?"

Eric melted into the shadows and without hesitation Melissa answered. "Bruce is helping me."

A man burst into the door's opening and Melissa fell back a step, releasing the door.

"And who are you?" The man asked, leading with a gun.

All Melissa could see was the black barrel pointed directly at her. Backpedaling, she shook her head.

Eric came out of the darkness, stepping between Melissa and the man. Before the man could react, Eric sliced his blade across the man's neck. The man's eyes flared as his mouth hinged open, then his hand went to his throat. Blood flowed over his fingers as he sank in the doorway, keeping the door from closing.

Although she'd known the plan, she was still stunned to see all the blood and how easily Eric had executed the plan, executed the *men*.

She inhaled sharply.

Eric glanced at her. "You okay?" His voice was whisper-quiet.

No, she was definitely not okay. Still, she nodded.

Eric tucked his knife into a sheath at his hip, then he waved Tyler and John over before grabbing the dead man under the arms and started dragging him out of the doorway. He looked at Melissa, then tilted his head toward the backpack on the ground. Understanding what he wanted, she half-lifted and half-dragged the pack into the doorway where she used it to prop the door open once the man was out of the way.

With all that Eric had just done for them, Melissa was almost ashamed that she'd thought for even a minute that he would double-cross them. He had done the complete opposite and she was extremely grateful, despite her shock.

Tyler and John joined them, and Eric motioned with his head that they should all step aside for a conversation.

"From my earlier recon," Eric said, his voice barely audible, "I don't think there are any more bad guys, but I'm not positive, so we need to use caution."

Wait. Was he suggesting they should all go in there? Where it was darker than a cave?

"I'll lead," he said as he withdrew a handgun from his hip. "Tyler follows, then John." He turned to Melissa. "You're only armed with a knife, so it's up to you whether or not you want to come in."

Relief flooded her. But then she glanced around. Was it any safer outside than in? Inside she wouldn't be alone, whereas outside, who knew who was lurking about, ready to harm her? Neither option was great, but she decided she would rather stay where there was enough illumination from the moon to allow her to see than go in there where the unknown terrified her.

"I'll wait here," she said.

Eric nodded, John smiled, but Tyler wore a grim expression, like he was completely focused on what he might have to do.

They slipped inside, leaving Melissa alone.

CHAPTER 18

Alex

After parking the truck tight up against a smashed car, Alex pocketed the keys and got out of the truck. He tossed his backpack onto his back, adjusted the gun at his waist, then slung his AR over his right shoulder.

"That was smart to make it look like the truck was part of the pile-up, Dad," Jason said with a grin.

Alex smiled. "Thanks. With any luck we'll be able to drive it home after we find Mom." Otherwise, it would be a really long walk, and now that it was dark, that idea was even less appealing. Even so, he'd decided to leave it unlocked. If someone wanted in, they were going to get in. No reason to come back to a broken window, because if someone looked inside and realized there was nothing worth taking, maybe they would just leave the truck alone.

"Do you really think we'll find her?" Jason asked.

Wanting to project positivity, Alex nodded. He didn't want to consider not finding her. "Got everything?"

Jason patted the gun at his hip and adjusted his jacket. "Yep."

"Okay. Let's move out."

Together, they squeezed by the pile-up, which was when Alex saw that there were still people in a few of the cars. But with blood splattering the windows, they were obviously dead.

Sighing at the tragedy of it all, he shook his head. The thing was, in the past he'd read articles about EMPs, so he knew what the experts had said. With everything using a computer chip down—and computer chips were used in nearly every facet of life nowadays—the fatality level would be extremely high. Maybe not right away, but with most vehicles no longer running food would no longer be delivered, and with no electricity water would be shut off, not to mention sewage treatment plants would no longer run.

Society was in the midst of a collapse that was going to take people back two hundred years. At least back then people knew how to survive without all the modern conveniences society had come to rely on.

Alex tried to recall specifically what the experts had said about the timeline of survival. One thing he'd read had stuck in his mind. They'd agreed that it would take up to ten years, maybe longer, to bring the power grid back online, and in that time ninety percent of the population would die from murder, starvation, dehydration, disease, and suicide, with the majority being killed in the first few months.

As that thought sunk in and Alex recognized that that scenario was no longer a theory but was now a reality, his heart started to stutter in his chest, and he found it hard to breathe.

"Are you okay, Dad?"

In the small amount of illumination from the moon, Alex could see the worry on his son's face, which only underlined his own despair. This new reality was what his children would grow up in. Assuming they survived.

They'd nearly made it past the pile-up, but Alex stopped and leaned against the hood of a silver Lexus. "I just need a minute."

Jason stared at Alex, tilting his head as his brow wrinkled. "Okay."

Alex leaned forward and rested his head in his hands, taking several deep breaths. As devastating as life was about to become—had already become—he had to get a grip. His family depended on him. He didn't have the luxury of falling apart. Especially now when Melissa could be in danger.

Dragging in a final breath, he straightened, then loudly exhaled before tossing Jason a smile. "I'm good now." He stood and gave a single nod. "Let's go."

Leading the way, Alex broke free of the tangle of cars and marched along the expressway with Jason by his side. The darkness closing in around them felt sinister somehow. The night was devoid of sound, except for an occasional shout and a smattering of dogs barking, but when a gunshot echoed in the distance, Alex struggled to keep a positive attitude.

When he'd gotten up that morning, he'd gotten ready for work, kissed Melissa goodbye, wished their children a good day, and driven away. Life had been ticking along the way it had every day of his life. And then the EMP had hit. Who knew who had done it? The United States had many enemies, several which had access to the materials needed to detonate a nuclear weapon high in the atmosphere and who would love to see America brought to her knees. Really though, did it matter who had done it? The more looming concern in Alex's mind was survival. He was just outside of Salt Lake City, a place he had always considered to be safe and friendly. Sure, it had its share of crime, but generally people seemed to care for one another. Society in the middle of collapse was changing that, and rapidly. He could only imagine what it was like in other parts of the country.

"What was that?" Jason whispered, yanking Alex out of his head.

Chagrined that he'd let his thoughts wander rather than paying attention to his surroundings, Alex scanned the area. They were approaching a turnoff to a neighborhood. A dog was barking frantically. Was that what Jason was talking about? Then he heard it. Someone had cried out. It sounded like a woman and it sounded like she was in distress.

Though his initial instinct was to see if she needed help, when he considered that Melissa might need him too, he hesitated.

What if it is Melissa?

Though that was unlikely, it tugged at him.

The woman cried out again, this time screaming, "Help! Someone help me! Please!"

Heaving a sigh, Alex looked at Jason, whose eyes were wide and filled with a mix of fear and desperation. "We should help her," Jason said.

Proud that his son would want to go to someone's aid, Alex had to nod his agreement. "All right. But we need to be cautious. It could be a trap. Or, at the very least, dangerous."

Jason nodded vigorously.

CHAPTER 19

Alex

LEADING THE WAY, Alex veered off of the road and trotted toward the neighborhood, keeping to the shadows. Jason was right behind him. Glad he'd left Steven and Emily at home—although he couldn't help but wonder how they were faring—Alex pressed himself against the wooden fence that surrounded the back of the house on the corner. A low chain-link fence ran along the side of the house. Not wanting to be exposed, but with no other way to approach, Alex crouched low and crab-walked along the sidewalk.

Another cry sounded on top of the barking dog. The good thing was, the sound helped him pinpoint the woman's location, which seemed to be down the street to their left. Dashing across the road, Alex listened intently for any other sounds, like a man's voice or a gunshot. He heard neither.

When he and Jason reached the other side of the street,

they crossed the grass on the house's side yard and pressed against the stucco exterior. A playset sat in the yard a short distance away, the swings motionless.

"No!" the woman's voice cried out. "Please! Leave me alone." Then sobbing.

Whatever was happening to the woman wasn't good. That was perfectly clear.

He turned to Jason, and in a low voice, said, "I'll go first. You back me up but stay hidden." Then, knowing he had to say it even though he didn't want to in the worst way, he added, "If you have to shoot someone…" he swallowed over the horror he felt. "Shoot to kill."

Jason stared at him a moment, then, mouth hanging open, nodded. "Right."

Desperately hoping it wouldn't come to that, Alex crept forward, staying in the shadows as much as he could. He unslung his AR, knowing it would be the best chance he would have to take someone down from a relatively safe distance. Glad he'd spent a fair amount of time at the shooting range and that he was quite comfortable with this rifle, he dashed to an oversized pine tree that sat between the house he'd been hiding next to and the neighboring house.

With someone's dog barking its head off, it was a little hard to hear, but there was no mistaking the whimpering. He peered around the tree. With no lights it was a little challenging to see, but his eyes were completely adjusted to the dark, so he managed to make out the front of the house and a carport on the other side of it. That's where it sounded like the commotion was coming from.

"Hold still and I won't hurt you," a man's voice said, sounding angry.

"You *are* hurting me! Let go!"

Alex glanced behind him to see where Jason was and saw his son where he'd left him. He motioned for him to join him. Moments later, Jason was there.

"You stay here," he said, his voice barely above a whisper. "I'm going to get closer."

"Be careful, Dad."

Nodding, Alex turned his attention to the house. Using the overgrown tree as cover, he backtracked to the opposite side of the tree, then dashed the short distance to the house before sliding along the front toward the carport. When he reached the place where the house ended and the carport began, he poked his head around then yanked it back, but in that brief moment he'd seen a man—he thought just one—kneeling over a woman lying on the ground. The man's back had been to him.

Wanting to make sure what he'd seen, Alex took a longer look. Yep. There was just the one man and it looked like he had bad intentions for the woman.

Gathering his nerve, Alex flicked on the flashlight attached to his AR and stepped out from cover. He led with his AR, the flashlight lighting up the man. "Back away." He made his voice as commanding as he could.

The man jerked, obviously surprised, spinning around to look at Alex. "This don't concern you, so beat it."

Really? He was going with that? Like Alex would walk away and let him assault a woman who was clearly at his mercy?

But what if Alex was misreading the whole thing? Maybe he had it all wrong, although something was definitely off. He shifted his eyes to the woman. "What's going on here? Do you know this man?"

She shook her head. "No." Her voice shook. "Please help me."

Okay. That cleared *that* up.

"Get away from her," Alex said. "I'm not going to ask a second time."

The man grinned, like he didn't believe Alex would actually do anything. "Do you even know how to use that thing?"

Clenching his jaw, Alex pulled back the charging handle then let it go, putting one in the chamber. "Do you really want to find out?"

The man's eyes widened and he turned away from the woman, who immediately scooted away from him. The man threw his hands up. "Okay, okay. No need to get nasty."

"On your feet."

The man stood.

"Any weapons?"

The man hesitated, then shook his head.

What was that hesitation all about? Was he lying?

Alex wanted to search him, but he would need Jason for

that. Not eager to involve his son, he didn't see any other way around it. Because he wasn't about to involve the woman, who was now cowering in a corner.

"Jason!"

His son materialized by his side in seconds. "Yeah, Dad?"

Keeping his AR trained on the man, Alex said, "Hands on your head." The man complied. "Now turn around."

The man glared at Alex but did as Alex commanded.

Not liking this one bit, Alex handed his AR to Jason. Although Jason had some training on the rifle, he had nowhere near as much practice as Alex had. Even so, Alex wasn't about to send his son to search the man.

"Cover me," he said, his voice barely audible.

Jason nodded.

Alex approached the man with caution. Even though he'd never done a pat down before, he was confident he could figure it out. Standing behind the man, Alex put his hands just under the man's arms, but the moment he began patting, the man spun around. Caught off guard, it took a moment for Alex to react, but by then, the man was tackling him.

"Dad!"

"Don't shoot!" Alex shouted, worried his son would shoot him by mistake.

Scuffling with the man on the concrete floor of the carport, Alex rolled onto his side. His gun pressed into his hip.

If he could just get to it...

Alex hadn't been in very many fights. Okay, maybe one

when he was in his twenties. So, his experience with hand-to-hand combat was extremely limited. However, the man he was fighting didn't seem all that experienced either. Probably only attacked women.

Although his experience was limited, Alex was in good shape—worked out regularly—and he was a hair over six feet. This man, on the other hand, didn't seem nearly as strong or as big.

Okay, then. Use that to your advantage.

With zero doubt that this could be a life or death situation—not only for him, but for his son, because if something happened to Alex, either this man would take Jason out or Jason would be left on his own on the streets—Alex felt a fresh rush of adrenaline flooding his body. He had to get the upper hand and fast.

With the man straddling his waist and Alex on his back, Alex bent his legs and placed his feet flat on the ground, then he grabbed the man's right arm and thrust his hips upward while twisting to his left. The man lost his center of gravity and fell over. Not wasting a moment, Alex leapt on top of him, pinning him, but the man didn't relent. Instead, he swung his arms, trying to gain the advantage. Alex tried to grab his wrists, but the man's arms were flailing around too much.

"Get off of me!" the man yelled, then he went for the gun at Alex's hip, which had revealed itself in the scuffle. The man's fingers wrapped around the Glock, but with the way it was on Alex's hip, the man was grabbing it backwards. Which meant if he got it out, he would only have to tilt it up for it to be pointed right at Alex. Even upside down it would be deadly.

Slightly panicked at how quickly things were going south, Alex grabbed the gun, which was nearly free of the holster, and gave it a twist, freeing it from the man's grasping hands. Managing to gain control of the weapon, Alex began turning it toward the man, but before he could get it aimed, the man grabbed the barrel and yanked it so that it was aimed at nothing. Not about to let the man take his weapon, Alex clung to the grip. The gun swung around wildly. Struggling to regain control, Alex slid his finger inside the trigger guard, and with one last effort, he pushed against the man's resistance until the gun was pointed at the man's head. Then, he reluctantly squeezed the trigger.

Boom!

His aim had been true. The man fell back, dead, blood pooling beneath his head.

Breathing heavily, Alex closed his eyes and shook his head. He'd not only killed one man that day, but two. He could hardly believe it. How had the world come to this already?

"Dad! Are you okay?"

Opening his eyes, Alex got off the man, then stood and faced his son. "Yeah." The dejection in his tone was clear.

Glancing around to make sure no other threats had appeared, when he didn't see anyone but his son and the woman, he tucked his gun into its holster and took the AR back from Jason, putting it over his shoulder. He didn't want his son to have the burden of taking anyone's life. Not if he could help it.

He turned to look at the woman. She'd gotten to her feet but stood a distance away in the far reaches of the dark carport.

"Are you all right?" Alex asked. "Did he hurt you?"

She shook her head. "I'm okay." She took several steps toward him as a tentative smile curved her lips. "Thanks to you." She paused. "I'm Misty."

He nodded. "I'm Alex." He turned to his son. "This is Jason." Glancing behind her, he asked, "Is this your house?"

She nodded. "Yes. I just came outside for a minute, to take out the trash, and he..." her eyes slid to the man before quickly going back to Alex, "he came out of nowhere and attacked me."

"I take it no one else is home."

She shook her head. "My husband, I don't know where he is."

How many other families were separated? Most people would have been at work when the EMP hit, meaning most people would have to get home on foot. Just like him. Just like Melissa.

He had to go. Had to find his wife. Who knew how many other people like the man he'd just shot were out there, looking for vulnerable people to attack? Now that law and order was gone and society was collapsing, people who had up until now controlled their evil natures would have to control themselves no more. Those people knew they could get away with anything now, which would only embolden them to do whatever evil deeds their heart's desired. Just like this man who had told Alex to mind his own business because he thought he could get away with doing whatever he wanted. Those were the kinds of people that would make this world a terrifying and dangerous place. That was a bigger threat than trying to find food and water.

Suppressing a shudder at their new reality, Alex said, "I hope he comes home." He paused. "We've got to go." He nodded toward Jason. "We're looking for my wife."

"Good luck to you."

"Thanks."

At that, they turned and strode away.

CHAPTER 20

Melissa

Now that she was all alone, Melissa was aware of every single sound—not that there were many. With everything electronic off all she heard were crickets chirping and dogs barking. Those didn't scare her. But when she heard gunshots, her heart raced. The sound wasn't coming from inside the Arctic Circle, but somewhere distant. Even so, it meant that bad things were happening, things that could eventually reach her. After all, she was still miles from home and night had fallen.

She couldn't stop her gaze from sliding to the dead men on the ground. Swallowing over the lingering distress that she couldn't seem to shake, she forced her eyes away. Instead, with her back to the wall, she let her gaze slowly scan the area surrounding this side of the Arctic Circle. Her vision had adjusted to the darkness, which allowed her to see far enough into the distance to keep an eye out for danger. Which is when she saw three men walking along the sidewalk, coming in her general direction. Had they seen her? She didn't think so. Their barely audible conversation was punctuated with raucous laughter, and although they looked around occasionally, their gaze hadn't yet landed on her.

As they drew closer, she saw that all three had handguns strapped to their waists and two of them had rifles slung over their shoulders. Were these good guys like Eric, or killers and kidnappers like the men sprawled on the ground near her? If they were armed and out at night, they couldn't have anything good in mind.

Desperate to stay out of their sight, she glanced toward the door that had been swung outward and propped open, then made a decision. Quickly and silently, she slid along the stuccoed wall until she reached the corner of the building farthest from the sidewalk. Peeking around the edge, she didn't see anyone, so she slipped around the side.

Eric, Tyler, and John had been inside for at least three minutes. Shouldn't they be coming out any second now? Hopefully with Tamara.

Peering back around the corner to where she'd been waiting moments before, she saw the trio of men pause on the sidewalk, their focus on the propped-open door. After a brief conversation that Melissa couldn't hear, they began crossing the grass.

Crap! They were going to investigate the Arctic Circle

which would put John, Tyler, and Eric—and Tamara—in mortal danger.

Desperate to warn her friends but terrified to call attention to herself, Melissa froze, her heart thrashing against her ribs.

What should I do? What should I do?

Thoughts flying, she got an idea.

She hurried to the other side of the Arctic Circle, the side where all the windows were, the side opposite where those three men had been headed. Cupping her hand against the glass, she peered in, but it was completely dark inside and she couldn't see a thing. With her chest tight with panic, she used the tip of one finger to lightly tap on the glass. Two seconds later, Tyler's face appeared.

Startled, it took Melissa a full second to regain her composure, then she held up three fingers and whisper-screamed, "Three men are coming!"

Tyler tilted his head and cupped his ear. She repeated her message, but he just shook his head.

Aw! He can't hear me!

Panic swelled to a crescendo.

Frantic to get her message across, but terrified to reveal her position, Melissa did the only thing she could think of. She repeatedly pointed her finger to the area behind Tyler. He must have gotten the message because he looked over his shoulder, then spun around. Half a second later Melissa heard a gunshot, and then Tyler's body fell against the glass before sliding out of view.

Gasping audibly, she dropped to her knees.

They just shot Tyler!

Her gaze darted in every direction for a place to hide, then she scrambled to get to the other side of the large drive-thru menu board. It wasn't much of a barrier to bullets, but it was better than nothing.

Several more gunshots rang out. She didn't want to even begin to consider that Eric and John—and perhaps Tamara—had been killed. Maybe her friends had gotten the upper hand, but she had no way of knowing. Instead, on her hands and knees, she crawled into the parking lot, making her way to the farthest car as fast as she could. Pressing her back against a tire, the water bottles in her backpack purse jabbing at her spine, she wrapped her arms around her bent knees in an attempt to make herself as small as she could.

Sitting there, waiting to somehow know when it was safe to come out, she felt wetness on her cheeks. Had she been shot? Was it blood? Swiping it away, she looked at her hands. No. It was tears. They were streaming down her face and she hadn't even realized it.

Using the knees of her pants, she wiped the tears from her cheeks, then she took slow, deep breaths in an effort to get control over herself. She had to have her wits about her. After all, it was highly possible that she was completely on her own now.

Her stomach twisted painfully at the notion and she thought she might throw up.

Swallowing convulsively, she concentrated all of her attention on her breathing. Well, almost all of it. Another part of her, the part that was meant to keep her alive, the part that controlled her fight or flight response, was finely attuned to any and all sounds, movement, and smells.

Rather shocked at how her mind and body had gone into survival mode, Melissa rested her cheek on her knees.

CHAPTER 21

Melissa

"Melissa," a voice called out a few minutes later, just loud enough for her to hear.

Her head shot up. Was that John?

Getting back on her hands and knees, she crawled toward the front of the car, then peered around. Yes! There was John! And he seemed unharmed.

Even so, once she got to her feet, she stayed cautious. "Over here," she called out just above a whisper.

In the moonlight, she saw a smile blossom on his lips. He waved her over.

While scanning her surroundings, Melissa hurried to his side. "You're okay?"

He nodded. "Yeah. So's Eric." His smile grew. "And Tamara."

After all that had happened, Melissa had started to

mentally prepare herself to learn that Tamara was dead. "Really?"

"Yeah. The men who took her gave her something to knock her out, but she's awake now."

"What about the..." she tried not to replay the memory of Tyler being shot but couldn't erase the image. "What about the men who shot Tyler?"

John grimaced. "They're dead." He hung his head. "And Tyler didn't make it."

Not surprised, although deeply saddened, Melissa felt tears threatening again. How had her world gone from steady and predictable to all-out bedlam in a matter of hours?

Which made her think about her family. Had Alex made it home? Were he and the children safe? Or had he gotten caught up in dangers of his own? Was he even still alive?

Don't think that way. Don't think that way.

Blowing out a steadying breath, Melissa forced her mind to focus on the here and now, on getting herself to a safe place.

"Come on," John said, gently taking her arm.

Blinking away the tears, Melissa nodded and let him lead her around the Arctic Circle back toward the side door. As they rounded the corner, she was thrilled to see Tamara sitting on the ground, her back against the wall. She was a fair distance from the dead men who had taken her, the men Eric had killed earlier.

Eric was standing guard, his eyes constantly moving.

"She's okay," John announced.

Eric looked at Melissa and gave a sharp nod, then went right back to keeping watch.

Melissa hurried to Tamara's side, hunkering down beside her. "Are you all right? Did they hurt you?"

Tamara shook her head and lifted her shoulders at the same time. "Not really. I mean, when I wouldn't stop fighting, they covered my mouth with a cloth that stunk of some chemical and I guess it knocked me out."

Melissa put her arms around her friend as fresh tears filled her eyes. "I'm so glad you're okay."

"Me too."

Melissa released her and sat on the ground beside her.

Tamara stared at her hands for several beats, then she met Melissa's gaze, her chin trembling. "I can't believe so many of our group is dead. And Tyler..." she shook her head. "He died because of me."

Laying her hand on Tamara's arm, Melissa shook her head. "It's not your fault."

"He wouldn't have died if he wasn't trying to rescue me."

"But it's not your fault those men took you."

Giving Melissa a sad smile, Tamara shifted her gaze to the ground. All Melissa could do was put an arm around Tamara's shoulders.

"You guys should find somewhere to spend the night," Eric said.

"I want to get home," Tamara said, lifting her eyes to Eric.

Eric shook his head. "It's not safe out."

No one disputed that. Not after all they'd been through.

Wait. Eric had said *You guys*. Was he not coming with them? Then again, why would he? He'd only come along when they needed him. It's not like he was looking to join their group.

"What are you going to do?" Melissa asked.

Eric turned to her. "I'm heading home."

"Where's home?" Tamara asked.

"North."

Since he didn't seem want to share more than that, Melissa just nodded. "Are you going to travel all night?"

He nodded. "If necessary."

"Thank you," Tamara said. "For everything."

He pushed away from the wall. "Best of luck to you." Then he strode toward the sidewalk, turned right, and disappeared from view.

With Eric gone, Melissa felt a fresh sense of danger. It was just her, Tamara, and John. Not exactly the most experienced group to be with. Then again, they'd managed to survive when so many of their number had not. But was it dumb luck, or had they done some things right?

"Eric took this off of Tyler," John said.

Turning her head to see what John was talking about, Melissa saw him holding out a gun. She got to her feet and faced him.

"I'm already armed," he said, "so, do you want it? Are you comfortable with guns?"

Melissa nodded. "Yeah." She took the gun from John. It was larger than her small pistol, but she was thrilled to have *something* with which to protect herself. "Thanks." She worked hard not to think about the fact that this gun had belonged to Tyler and what she had witnessed happen to him.

"Eric took this off of Tyler too," John said with a small frown.

Melissa took the waist holster from John, glad she would have a way to comfortably carry the gun. Putting it in the pocket of her slacks wouldn't be the best option. She hooked the holster on the inside of her waistband and slid the gun inside. It felt a bit unnatural to have that bulge at her hip, but in a way it was also comforting, because she knew she could defend herself. At least if she had enough time to draw before being attacked. She would just have to stay hyper-alert.

"We should get going," John said.

Extremely relieved that she wasn't by herself, Melissa nodded, then she reached down to Tamara and helped her friend to her feet.

"Where should we go?" Tamara asked, her eyes tight with worry.

"I don't know," Melissa said. She could only imagine how vulnerable she would feel if she'd been the one kidnapped. Even though nothing had happened to Tamara beyond being rendered unconscious, all kinds of terrible things probably would have happened if Eric, John, and Tyler hadn't gone after her. Melissa knew that she needed to do everything within her power to make sure she wasn't ever taken.

CHAPTER 22

Melissa

"Let's just start walking south," John suggested. "We'll look for a safe place to spend the night as we're heading home."

Melissa liked the idea of holing up somewhere during the night and facing the world when the sun was shining again. The bright light of a fresh day always made things seem a little less dire. Of course, that was when her world had been normal and predictable. Now, the new day could look just as a harrowing as the night. And that was assuming they made it to morning. After seeing four of their group murdered, Melissa had no assurances that any of them would live to see the sun rise.

Rather than share her fears, she nodded. "Yeah. Okay." Shifting her eyes to Tamara, she asked, "What about you? Are you up for some walking?"

"I don't have much choice, do I?"

"No. I guess you don't."

"Then let's go." She glanced at her sneakers. "At least we have comfortable shoes."

Melissa laughed, but when she thought of their foray into that shoe store earlier that day, she had to shake her head. It seemed like ages ago.

They set off, walking along the sidewalk, staying to the shadows as much as possible. Melissa brushed a hand against the gun at her hip, feeling slightly reassured that she could defend herself if it came to that.

"Let's cross the street," John said a short time later.

Melissa looked at the other side of the eight-lane road. Thick trees blotted out any moonlight. A chill ran through her. "Why do you want to go over there?"

John glanced around. "I feel kind of exposed on this side. Those trees will provide some cover. Or at least a way to hide if someone comes along."

"Or someone could be hiding in there," Tamara pointed out, which was exactly what Melissa had been thinking.

John looked from Melissa to Tamara. "I just…I want to keep you both safe."

Touched by the sincerity in his tone and knowing all he'd done that day, like going into the Arctic Circle to rescue Tamara, Melissa smiled. "I appreciate that."

"Me too," Tamara said. She peered across the street. "I guess it makes sense to, you know, have a place to hide if we think there's trouble."

Melissa didn't love it, but being out in the open the way they were wasn't ideal either. She nodded. "Let's do it."

Together, the three of them crossed the street, making their way between the stalled cars until they reached the other side. When they stepped onto the sidewalk, Melissa studied the overgrown foliage beside the sidewalk. Nothing stirred, but when she imagined someone hiding in the brush, a shiver raced through her. Or maybe it was the cold night air. She pulled her sweater tighter around her, but it did little to warm her. At least there was a split-rail fence separating the bushes from the sidewalk. That would make it a little harder for someone to jump them. Unless the person had a weapon. Then they could shoot them from cover.

Stop thinking of the worst that can happen. What if nothing happens at all? What if you make it home and find Alex and the kids safe and sound?

Since that was the option she desperately wished for, she forced herself to visualize that happening instead of something awful.

They plodded on but had yet to see a place they thought would work for spending the night.

"Someone's coming!" Tamara whisper-screamed, pointing in the direction they were headed.

Melissa narrowed her eyes, her gaze scanning. A moment later she saw them. Two men walking along the sidewalk across the street. One of them had a rifle over his shoulder. Memories of what had happened at the Arctic Circle a short time before slammed through Melissa, sending a tremor of fear right to the heart of her.

Desperate to not be seen, she said, "Let's hop the fence and hide in the bushes."

Tamara and John nodded.

Melissa looked at the fence, which had three white, horizontal slats of wood with wide gaps between them. Shouldn't be too hard to climb over. It was more of a decorative fence than anything else.

Melissa and Tamara climbed over without too much difficulty. John, being the large man that he was, had a bit more trouble, but he made it over as well. The three of them pushed backwards into the bushes, although the foliage was too thick for them to get very deep. Even so, Melissa felt pretty well hidden.

Glad that she and Tamara had listened to John's suggestion to cross the street, she watched the two men as they made their way north. Between the eight lanes separating her from the men and the darkness, it was hard to see them very well, but in the absolute stillness of the night, she could make out their quiet conversation.

"Hey, Dad," one of the men said, which surprised Melissa. It was a father and son? "Maybe we should go back. I mean, there's no one around."

The other man stopped and looked at his companion, but then his head turned like he was searching, searching. His gaze tracked toward her, Tamara, and John. He paused as he looked their way, which sent Melissa's heart slamming, but then his eyes moved past them as if he hadn't seen them. She exhaled in relief, although her heart still stuttered.

Despite the darkness and distance, something about the man seemed familiar. In a way he reminded her of Alex. But there was no way it could be Alex. All the way here? It was too far from home.

No. It was just her heart's desire to be reunited with her family that was trying to convince her of something that wasn't there.

"Maybe you're right, Jason," the man said.

Melissa's eyes flared with shock. He'd called the other person Jason, right? She hadn't misheard? And this Jason, he'd called the other man Dad.

No. It couldn't be. No way.

The pair turned around and began walking back the way they'd come. And they were moving fast. Like whatever they'd come to do hadn't panned out and now they wanted to get back to where they'd started.

Could it have been Alex and Jason out looking for her?

Her hope for that outcome was so profound that she nearly called out to the men. But what if she was wrong? What if they were like the men who had killed so many of her friends? She couldn't risk it. Not after all she'd witnessed, all that she'd experienced.

"That was close," Tamara whispered from beside her.

"We have to follow them," Melissa said, having made the decision without even realizing it. She turned and faced Tamara and John.

"What?" Tamara's tone said she thought Melissa was nuts. "I'm not following those men." There was no room for negotiation in Tamara's voice.

"But I think...it might be my husband and son."

"What makes you think that?" John asked, his voice coming from the bushes like a ghost.

"Didn't you hear what they said? One was named Jason and the other said Dad. My son's name is Jason."

Tamara recoiled slightly. "You're going to risk our lives because a man has the same name as your son? Really?"

"So, you heard him say Jason?"

She shook her head. "I didn't hear anything."

Melissa looked at John, who had stepped out of the bushes. "What about you?"

"I couldn't hear anything."

Had she misheard? Had she been so desperate for it to be true that her ears were playing tricks on her?

She replayed the incident.

When she'd heard the man call his companion Jason, she'd had no thought that it could be her husband and son. That idea hadn't come to her until *after* she'd heard the first man call the other man Jason.

"I'm going," she said. The men were nearly out of sight. "You guys wait here. I just have to get close enough to find out." She began climbing the fence.

"Don't go," Tamara said, grabbing her arm.

Melissa paused. "I have to."

Even in the dim moonlight, Melissa could see the terror in Tamara's eyes.

"I'll be fine," she said, although she had no reassurance of that. "I won't let them see me."

"We'll keep walking," John said, "but if you don't come back..." he grimaced, "I can't promise we'll be able to help you."

That was fair. Melissa nodded. "If it's them, we'll come back for you."

Tears shimmered in Tamara's eyes. "Be safe."

Melissa gave her a small smile, then she clambered over the fence.

CHAPTER 23

Alex

ALEX DIDN'T WANT to feel like he was giving up, but he kind of was. After Jason had suggested they go back and had pointed out that no one was around, it seemed rather fruitless to keep walking. They could cover more ground in the truck heading south, which was the direction it made more sense to be looking in anyway. That was the way home, after all.

Then why had he felt the urge to go this way? Well, he *had* saved Misty. And killed a man. But the man had been about to assault Misty. Maybe that had been the reason he'd felt spurred on somehow to go the way they had. But now they'd wasted all kinds of time that could have been spent searching for Melissa.

Sighing with resignation, Alex had to push himself to keep pace with Jason, who seemed eager to get back to the truck. Well, Alex was eager too. The sooner they got there, the sooner they could search another area, because Alex didn't want to come home without Melissa.

What if she's already there? Maybe she's home worrying about you. Maybe you should go home.

Shaking off the thought, he reminded himself to stay aware.

Moments later he thought he heard something.

"Slow down," he murmured to Jason.

"What's up?"

"Shhh. Don't turn around, but I thought I heard something. Keep moving but go slower. And listen."

Jason gave a brisk nod but slowed.

Alex's ears strained to hear any little sound. A dog barked in the distance. A shout could be heard somewhere far off.

There!

He heard it again. A shuffling sound, like someone was trying to sneak up on them. He swung his AR off of his shoulder and spun around. Nothing. No one there. But cars littered the road. Someone could be hiding behind any one of them. Someone could be going from car to car, pacing them.

He flicked on his flashlight, reluctant to kill again, but willing to if it came to that. He wasn't about to be anyone's victim.

He met Jason's eyes and signaled with his head to go behind a nearby tree. Jason complied.

Satisfied that his son was safe, Alex stepped into the road, leading with his AR. He eased along the back of a black SUV, pausing when he reached the corner of it. The windows were tinted so he couldn't see through to the other side. Then again, whoever was following him and Jason—if someone was following them—wouldn't be able to see him either.

Unless they were looking under the SUV's chassis.

Not wanting to be caught unaware, he knelt on the pavement, then bent forward and did a quick visual sweep of the area near the SUV. No feet were visible, and it was too dark to see much beyond this vehicle.

Standing, he sighed and shook his head. Maybe he'd imagined the whole thing. But did he want to gamble on that? No. Not when his son's life was also on the line.

He stepped around the back of the SUV, his AR still up and ready, although his finger was outside the trigger guard. The flashlight lit up the area. Advancing steadily forward, whenever Alex reached a vehicle, he took a moment to check all around it, slowly clearing the area.

Movement to his right caught his eye. He spun toward it. Someone was there. He knew it.

"Let me see your hands," he said in a commanding tone. When nothing happened, he narrowed his eyes and slid his finger closer to the trigger, although still outside the trigger guard. "I know you're there and I don't want to shoot you, but I will if I have to. Now, show yourself. Hands first."

A pair of hands slowly lifted from the other side of a compact car. They were small, like a woman's hands. Or a small man? Maybe a teenager. Light glinted off a ring on the person's left ring finger. A diamond ring. Definitely a woman.

Why was she following him? Was she alone? Or was she a distraction before an ambush?

Alarmed, he adjusted his aim. "Are you alone?" he called out. When there was no response, he got more worried. "Answer me!"

"Alex?" a tentative voice called out.

Alex recoiled. *What the heck?*

"Show yourself," he demanded as he refocused through his scope.

Slowly, the top of a head appeared, then a face.

Alex's mouth fell open and he staggered back a step, his hands automatically shifting his AR so that it pointed to the pavement.

"Melissa?" His voice was filled with disbelief.

"Alex!" She ran toward him.

He slung his AR over his shoulder and raced to her. A moment later she was in his arms. He couldn't believe it! He'd found her! He'd actually found her! Okay, maybe she'd found him. Wait. How had she found him?

Holding her tight against him, his heart felt like it might burst from happiness and relief.

"Mom!" Jason said as he joined them.

Alex pulled him into the group hug and tried to control the tears that pushed against the backs of his eyes.

"I knew it was you," she said against his shoulder. "I knew it."

After a long and wonderful embrace, Alex released her, and she stepped back. A radiant smile lit her face as she beheld him, then she turned to Jason, her smile just as bright. She lifted her eyes to Alex. "Where are Emily and Steven? Are they all right?"

He nodded. "They're safe and sound at home." At least he assumed they were. He desperately hoped they were.

She nodded.

"How did you find us?" he asked.

"I'll tell you," she said, "but we have to go back to get Tamara and John."

He'd met Tamara before, but he didn't remember John. "Back where?"

She turned and pointed the way they'd come, the way he and Jason had been going when they'd basically given up on finding her.

Startled to realize that they could have given up a little too soon and then this reunion wouldn't have happened, Alex felt a jolt. But it *had* happened, so there was no reason to think of what could have happened.

"Okay. Lead the way."

She intertwined her fingers with his and he clung to her hand. They got out of the street and onto the sidewalk, across from where they'd been walking earlier.

"They shouldn't be far," she said. "They said they were going to keep going."

As they walked, she gave a brief explanation of how she'd seen him and Jason coming their way, how she and her friends had hidden, how she'd thought it might be them, and how she'd followed them. "After what Tamara went through, I can't blame her for not wanting to follow you, but I had to know." She smiled at him again.

Alex released her hand and put an arm around her shoulders, tugging her against him. He never wanted to let her out of his sight again. He wondered what Melissa was talking about though, about what Tamara had been through. He wondered what Melissa had been through. He knew what he'd experienced. He hoped nothing like that had happened to her.

There would be time to discuss their day later. Right now, they needed to get her friends, get back to the truck, and get home.

"There they are," Melissa said, pointing to a man and a woman a short distance away.

"Tamara," she called out in a soft voice. "John. It was them. I knew it was them."

Her friends sped up and moments later Melissa was introducing Alex and Jason to John. Alex shook his hand and said hello to Tamara.

"We have a truck," Alex announced. "About a mile south of here. We would have driven it but there was a pile-up we couldn't get past."

"You have a truck?" Melissa asked. "Where'd you get a truck?"

Oh yeah. She had no idea what had happened. "I'll explain it to you later. Let's just get to it so we can all get home."

"You'll take me home?" Tamara asked.

He nodded, so happy that things had turned out well. "Of course. And John too."

She smiled. "Thank you."

"Yeah," John said. "That would be awesome."

"Let's get moving," Alex said.

CHAPTER 24

Melissa

IN A DAY OF HORRIFYING LOWS, finding her husband and son had been the most amazing high. Melissa couldn't stop smiling, and she didn't want to let go of Alex's hand. The strength in his grip was reassuring. No longer did she have to worry about where he was. Not when he was right beside her. As was Jason. Although she was thrilled to see her son, she would have preferred that he was safe at home with her two younger children. And she hadn't missed the fact that Jason was armed. Hating the idea that her seventeen-year-old son was carrying a gun, she was glad that she and Alex had taken the time to bring him shooting. If he had to be armed, at least he would know what he was doing, but she *hated* the idea that being armed had become a necessity.

"How far?" Tamara asked as the five of them plodded along.

"Not much farther," Alex said, the timbre of his voice filling Melissa with all kinds of warm feelings. Although she'd proven that she could take care of herself—at least she had so far—she always preferred to be with her husband and her children. No question.

They reached a tangle of cars. Even in the darkness it was clear that this had been a serious accident. Vehicles were smashed together. One large truck was even halfway on top of a small car. No wonder Alex and Jason hadn't been able to get through and had had to go on foot.

"Oh no," Alex said, his voice sinking.

"What?" Melissa asked. "What's wrong?"

"The truck's gone," Jason said.

Shoulders sagging, Melissa exhaled audibly. She was *so* tired. Exhausted, really. Until that moment, she hadn't realized how eager she'd been to stop walking and get a ride in a vehicle.

"Someone must have hot-wired it," Alex said.

"What are we going to do now?" Tamara asked, shivering in the cold night air.

"Keep walking?" John said.

Melissa turned to Alex. "I don't think I can make it all the way home tonight. I'm so dang tired." She glanced around, "I also don't like the idea of being out here all night."

"Plus," Tamara added, "It's freezing out here."

"You know," Melissa said, "when we crossed paths with you, we were actually looking for a place to shelter for the night."

Alex nodded. "I know a safe place where we can spend the night."

Surprised, Melissa asked, "Where?"

Alex shifted his gaze to Jason, whose eyebrows rose before he slowly nodded. Alex said, "Are you thinking what I'm thinking?"

Jason smiled. "Misty?"

"Yep."

"Who's Misty?" Melissa asked. She didn't know anyone by that name. Was it a friend of Jason's?

Alex turned to Melissa. "She's a woman we helped earlier. She lives close by."

Curious what had happened, but knowing this wasn't the time to ask for details, Melissa instead asked, "Do you think she'll let us stay at her house?"

He shrugged. "Only one way to find out."

All five of them turned around and began backtracking. Not long after, a turnoff to a neighborhood appeared.

"It's this way," Alex said. "The second house on the left."

When they reached the house, Alex faced the group. "I don't want to scare her, so Melissa and I will go to the door alone."

Everyone nodded their agreement, and with her hand in her husband's, Melissa began walking up the driveway. A dark puddle near the carport caught Melissa's eye. It seemed to be partially dried. Wait. Was that blood?!

With a quick glance at Alex, Melissa couldn't help but speculate what might have happened, and the memory of seeing Eric slash the throats of the men who'd kidnapped Tamara was fresh on her mind. Would the horrors of the day never end?

Quietly shaking her head, she briefly closed her eyes. No. They wouldn't. The world had changed now. Irrevocably and in the worst way.

They reached the front door.

"Misty," Alex called out in a quiet voice, although in the dead of night the sound surely carried. He followed that up with a gentle knock. "Misty, it's Alex. From earlier."

Melissa heard footsteps approaching on the other side of the door, then the door opened, and in the shadows stood a woman. Her eyes went from Alex to Melissa, then back to Alex. "You found your wife?"

Alex nodded, and when Melissa looked at his face, she couldn't miss the happiness shining from his eyes. "Yes."

The woman—Misty—looked past his shoulder. "Where's your son? Is he okay?"

"Yes. He's on the sidewalk with two other people. Co-workers of my wife's."

Misty shook her head. "Why are you here?"

"Our truck, someone took it. We were wondering..." he paused a beat. "Would it be all right if we spent the night here? We would leave first thing in the morning, but we don't want to be out all night and we have miles to go before we reach home."

She didn't even hesitate. Instead, she stepped back and

opened her door wide. "Yes, of course." Several candles burned in the room behind her.

Alex smiled. "Thank you. Let me just get Jason and the others."

While Alex went to gather the rest of their group, Melissa smiled at the woman. "I'm Melissa."

"Misty."

"We really appreciate this. I've…" she swallowed over the lump in her throat. "I can't deal with what's out there right now. I just need…" Tears leapt into her eyes, taking her by surprise. She shook her head.

Misty reached out and touched her arm. "I understand. Please, come in."

Exceedingly grateful for Misty's willingness to host perfect strangers in this dreadful time, Melissa impulsively gave her a hug. To her surprise, after a moment, Misty started sobbing. Melissa held her tight, her heart going out to her. Whatever had prompted those tears, Melissa was sure she could relate.

By the time Alex and the others had gone into the house, Misty's sobs had slowed, and Melissa gently released her. "Are you all right?"

Misty nodded once, then she began shaking her head. "My husband never came home."

Oh yeah. Melissa could totally relate. Ever since the EMP had obliterated modern society, Melissa had worried about Alex. She knew she had been so very blessed to be reunited with him.

"He's probably on his way home now," Melissa said as she kept her eyes locked on Misty's.

"That's what I keep telling myself, but I can't help but worry."

Melissa gave her a small smile. "It's not like he can just jump in a car and drive home. Even if he had a working car, the roads are a mess and..." she was about to say that coming straight home might not be a possibility with all the craziness out there, but she knew that wouldn't be helpful.

"And what?"

She shook her head. "It just takes longer to get home, that's all."

Misty sighed, like she'd resigned herself to waiting. "Well, I have to admit, I'm glad to not be alone."

Melissa chuckled. "Then I guess us staying here is a win-win."

Nodding, Misty turned to the group, who was standing around in her small living room. "I don't have much food, but if you're hungry, I'm willing to share."

"That's very generous," Alex said, "but we don't want to take your food." He took a pack off of his back. "I have some snacks in here."

"It's the least I can do," Misty said, then she shifted her eyes to Melissa. "Your husband and son saved me earlier."

Melissa's eyebrows rose. Alex had just said he'd helped her, not saved her. She would definitely have to get the details later.

"I just feel bad that he had to kill that man," Misty murmured.

Whoa! What? Alex had *killed* someone? Remembering the puddle of blood on the driveway, she turned to look at her husband. In the candlelight she could see his frown. She knew him well enough to know he wasn't happy he'd had to do whatever it was he had done, but for Misty's sake, she was glad he'd had the courage to do it.

"I'm super tired," Tamara said.

"Oh," Misty said, "right. Uh, I have two extra bedrooms up here and two in the basement. Not all of them have beds though. You guys can figure out who sleeps where." She took a flashlight from a side table. "Whoever goes in the basement will need this."

John took it from her. "Thank you for letting us stay the night."

Misty nodded.

Before long they'd sorted out the sleeping arrangements, with John and Tamara taking the two basement bedrooms, Alex and Melissa taking the guest bedroom on the main floor that had a queen bed, and Jason throwing a sleeping bag on the floor of the remaining guest bedroom.

In bed, Melissa snuggled into Alex's arms, her thoughts on her two younger children. They were all alone at the house. They had to be frightened. Especially Emily. Even though she was fifteen, she still wasn't a fan of the dark.

"I'm worried about Steven and Emily," she said. She could feel Alex nodding.

"I told them to go to Stan's house if they were scared," he said.

Grateful for good neighbors, that eased Melissa's mind some. "I'm sure they're worried about us. I wish there was some way to let them know we're okay. And to know they're okay."

"Right? I miss cell phones."

So did Melissa. And there was so much more she missed. Like the feeling of safety that she'd taken for granted. Would that ever return? She didn't want to think about the answer because she already knew what it was.

CHAPTER 25

Alex

WEAK SUNLIGHT FILTERED in through the window, waking Alex. For a moment he was disoriented. This wasn't his bedroom, although Melissa was sleeping next to him. Then it all came back to him. The EMP. The struggle to get home. Killing two people. Searching for Melissa. Finding Melissa. The truck being gone. Going to Misty's house.

Frowning deeply, he considered the day ahead. He figured their house was about ten miles away. If they kept a steady pace, it would take four or five hours. Barring anything terrible happening, which he knew was entirely possible, they should be home by early afternoon.

Feeling optimistic, he stretched, then gently shook Melissa. "Wake up, sleepyhead."

"Huh?" she murmured through half-closed eyes. "Did I oversleep? What time is it?"

CHRISTINE KERSEY

"No idea, but we should get going."

"Are the kids going to be late for..." her words trailed off as her eyes snapped open. "Oh no. I thought it was just a nightmare." She pushed up onto her elbows. "But it's not, is it?" She looked around the unfamiliar room, then turned to Alex.

He wished he could tell her it was only a nightmare, but it was all too real. "Yeah."

She sat up straight and lifted her chin. "Then let's go. I want to get home to our children."

Proud of her fortitude, he kissed her softly on the lips, then threw back the covers, got out of bed, and quickly dressed before going into the living room. To his surprise, Jason was already up. Normally one to sleep in as long as possible, Jason was chatting with Misty and a man Alex hadn't seen before. Had Misty's husband come home?

"Alex," Misty said, wearing a big smile, "this is Chris. My husband."

Alex shook the man's hand. "Glad you made it home."

Chris clasped both of Alex's hands in his. "I can't thank you and your son enough for coming to Misty's rescue yesterday." With a resolute nod, he released Alex's hand.

"Right time and place," Alex said.

"But you didn't have to help." With a tilt of his head and raised eyebrows, Chris added, "No one else did."

Glad he had, Alex didn't want to focus on that any longer. "Well, it all worked out, I guess."

Melissa, John, and Tamara joined them. After all the introductions, Alex said, "We have a ways to go, so we'd better get a move on. Thanks again for letting us crash here last night." He glanced at his group. "I don't know about the rest of you, but after a decent night's sleep, I feel a lot better." Although that was relative. He was still extremely worried about how their journey home would go, but at least they would have daylight, which would help them see trouble coming before it hit them. He hoped.

"Do you have everything you need?" Chris asked.

"A working vehicle would be nice," he said with a wry smile.

"Sorry. Can't help you there."

"Didn't think so. Other than that, I think we're good." He wasn't about to take any of Chris and Misty's supplies. They would need them, and Alex and his group weren't that desperate. Yet.

They said their goodbyes, then headed out the door. Gray clouds filled the sky. Was a snowstorm on the way? He hoped not. That would make the walk home that much more miserable.

It didn't take long to reach the same place where they'd turned back the night before. The truck Alex had left parked in a way he'd thought was so clever was still nowhere to be seen. Good thing they were all healthy enough to hoof it. Well, except maybe John. Alex had noticed that he'd been struggling a bit with the pace Alex was trying to set. But he'd made it from Melissa's office to this point so far. And he'd helped to keep Melissa safe. So, Alex would do whatever he could to help John get home.

They weaved their way through the mess of cars and continued on. When they got to the intersection of Van Winkle Expressway and 900 East, Alex stopped. "Okay. So, I'm thinking we go south on 900 East." He turned to Tamara and then John. "How would that work for getting to your houses?"

John nodded. "Yeah, that would be good. I can break off and head east when I get closer to my place."

"I don't live too far from you," Tamara said to John. "So, I'll break off when you do."

"Awesome," Alex said. "Let's keep moving. The sooner we get home, the better." He smiled at Melissa, who he could tell was chomping at the bit to get home to Steven and Emily.

"At least this brisk pace keeps us warm," John said with a chuckle.

Alex guessed it wasn't much above freezing, but if a storm began, it wouldn't warm much. He was just glad they'd had a warm place to sleep the night before. He didn't want to think about what might have happened if they'd had to be out all night.

Shoving aside those thoughts, he pushed on, walking on the shoulder of the road since there was no sidewalk in this area. The back of an apartment complex was to their right, and to their left was a low-slung office building. No one else seemed to be around, which was a relief. The fewer people they ran into the better, as far as Alex was concerned.

Passing through a residential area, they went about a mile without incident. Until they reached a shopping center where people were looting a sporting goods store. As they got closer, Alex could see people carrying out sleeping bags and other camping supplies, and a couple had rifles, probably liberated from the store.

Hefting his AR on his shoulder, he remembered how he'd had to kill two people the day before. He had yet to tell Melissa about it, and they hadn't discussed what they'd been through—they'd both been too exhausted to talk. There would be plenty of time for that later.

"More looters," Melissa said from beside him.

Alex turned to her. "You're not surprised, are you?"

She shook her head. "No." She glanced at the shoes on her feet, then grimaced at him. "I guess I'm a looter too. I took these sneakers yesterday. But only because I was getting blisters with my other shoes. And I only took them without paying because there was no one there to pay."

He put an arm around her and tugged her against him, wishing the worst he had done was take a pair of shoes.

CHAPTER 26

Melissa

As they walked by the shopping center, Melissa couldn't help but feel anxious. The day before she and her group had been minding their own business—okay, maybe they'd been checking out that dead body—when those guys had opened fire on them, killing three of their number and taking Tamara.

Speaking of Tamara, Melissa looked at her friend and saw her eyes shifting from side to side like she expected to be attacked at any moment. Melissa knew how she felt.

She turned her attention back to the looters. Not able to tear her gaze from the people coming and going in a frenzy, she said, "Let's go a little faster."

"Something wrong?" Alex asked as he turned to her.

"It's just, uh, all those people are making me nervous." The thought of someone firing on them—on her husband and son—made Melissa's apprehension climb several notches.

"All right," Alex said. "Sure. We can go faster." He looked toward John, who was panting a bit. "You okay?"

John nodded. "I'll be fine. And I agree with Melissa. Especially after what happened yesterday."

So, it wasn't unreasonable for her to have a bit of PTSD in regard to what she'd experienced. It had been terrifying.

"What happened yesterday?" Alex asked her.

With a glance at Jason, Melissa decided to share what she'd been through, even though she didn't like the idea of her son having to hear about such awful things. Then again, she didn't have to get into all the gory details.

With their quicker pace, they were soon beyond the shopping center and into another residential area where things were quiet. They slowed a bit, and as they walked, Melissa gave an abbreviated version of her trek the day before, leaving out the way Eric had slashed the men's throats and how she'd seen Tyler fall against the glass as he was shot.

Dang, why did she have to think about that?

Instead, she kept it simple, telling Alex that Rob, Dillon, and Curtis had been gunned down for no reason and how Eric had come along at the right time to help them free Tamara, and that Tyler had died in the process.

When she finished, Alex stopped and pulled her into his arms. "I wish I'd been there," he murmured.

Although she agreed, a part of her was glad he hadn't been. If he had been there, he could have been killed. But it would have been wonderful to have him by her side.

No matter. He was with her now.

He released her and they began walking again, then he turned to Tamara and John. "You guys are amazing. All of you."

Tamara smiled. "*They* are amazing. For rescuing me."

Melissa reached over and gave Tamara's arm a squeeze.

A gunshot rang out.

With her heart going into a gallop, Melissa dove to the pavement, then she immediately lifted her eyes to Jason and Alex to make sure they hadn't been shot. They looked healthy, just startled, as they hit the ground too. John and Tamara had also gotten down but looked unharmed.

"Where'd that come from?" Jason asked.

"Don't know," Alex said. "But I don't think it was meant for us."

All five of them crawled behind a car, which was way too reminiscent of the day before. Melissa's stomach churned with agitation as she shivered from the cold.

Another gunshot.

Melissa shuddered. The idea that walking along the street could be deadly—something that would have been ludicrous just twenty-four hours earlier—made Melissa shake her head in disbelief. But she had to believe it because it was all too accurate now. Sure, in some places in the country it might have been the way it was before, but not in Melissa's world. It was hard to wrap her head around.

"I never heard those rounds hitting anything," Alex pointed out. "I think the shots are somewhere inside that apartment complex."

"Good point, Dad," Jason said.

"So," Melissa began, "what? We just get up and keep walking like nothing happened?"

Alex scrubbed a hand over his face. "Do you have a better idea?"

They could wait there for a while, but that wouldn't guarantee their safety. And really, she wanted to get away from whatever was happening. She shook her head. "No. I don't."

Wearing a pained expression, he said, "Let's stay behind cars where possible until we're clear of this area."

With Alex leading the way, they crept forward, moving from stalled car to stalled car until they'd gone halfway down the block, then they stood and hustled forward before getting onto the sidewalk. There really wasn't anywhere to take cover, but they kept a steady pace. While staying aware of her surroundings, Melissa thought about her goal—getting home. That spurred her on.

Melissa walked beside Alex, Jason was behind them, and Tamara and John trailed a short distance behind Jason.

They began passing a 7-11 convenience store. The windows were smashed out and Melissa could see a few people inside. She doubted much was left on the shelves. Which made her think about her own pantry.

"How long do you think our food will last?" she asked Alex.

"Well, with that food storage Stan suggested we get we should be okay for a few months. Plus, the kids and I made a trip to the store yesterday to get a bit more. Really though, it's water I'm more concerned about."

Oh yeah. She hadn't even thought about water.

"I mean," he went on, "we have six of those fifty-five gallon drums Stan talked us into getting that we filled with water. And boy am I glad we let him convince us to get them. But they won't last forever." He grimaced at Melissa. "Daily showers are now a thing of the past."

Melissa hated when she got sticky with sweat, but being able to drink was more important than being squeaky clean.

"Wait," she said, "you said you went to the store with the kids yesterday. You mean, after you got home?"

He nodded. "We walked to the store and picked up what we could. On the walk home is when I, uh, I acquired that truck."

Glad he'd had the presence of mind to make a run to the store for a few more supplies, she said, "You never did tell me how you got the truck."

His footsteps seemed to grow heavy and his face became downcast.

Something bad had happened, clearly. Not sure she wanted to know now, Melissa said, "It's okay. You don't have to tell me."

He shifted his gaze to her as a sad smile barely lifted the corners of his mouth. "No. You should know. I mean, since the kids were there to witness it all."

Her children had been part of what had happened? Based on Alex's body language, Melissa knew it was bad. But knowing her sweet children had been there made her heart grow heavy with apprehension. "Tell me."

"When we were walking up the hill toward home, pushing our full grocery carts, some guy in a beat-up truck pulled up beside us and said he wanted what we'd just bought from the store. I told him no and to move on, and..." his voice trailed off.

"What?"

"When he insisted we give him what we had, I, uh, I pulled my gun on him. To encourage him to leave."

Rather shocked to imagine her husband drawing on someone, Melissa said, "Then what?"

"Then the man pointed a gun at Jason and said if I didn't lower my gun and load everything into his truck, he'd shoot Jason."

Melissa gasped. "Oh no." Even though this was something that had already happened and Jason hadn't been hurt, she still felt her heart race. "What did you do?"

"I acted like I was complying with his demand to put my gun down, then I..." he lowered his eyes, then glanced at Melissa. "I shot him."

Horrified, but also grateful Alex had protected Jason and their other children, Melissa took his hand. "Did the man... did he die?"

"Yeah," Alex said, his voice dropping.

"It was my idea to take the truck," Jason said as he moved up beside Melissa, obviously having overheard the conversation.

Melissa turned to him but didn't know what to say.

"I figured," Jason added, "the man didn't need it anymore and it would help us to find you."

With a shaky smile, she nodded. "Right. Makes sense."

"And we did find you," Alex said, giving her hand a gentle squeeze.

That was without dispute. Melissa smiled at him, then remembered the puddle of blood at Misty's house. "What happened with Misty?"

When a shadow fell over Alex's face, Melissa felt her insides twist with dread.

CHAPTER 27

Alex

ALEX WAS surprised Melissa had taken the story of his killing the man in the truck so well. What would she think of him when she learned that he'd killed not one, but *two* men the day before?

"When we came to the roadblock," he began, knowing he should just get it over with and hope for the best, "we parked the truck and set out on foot."

"We heard a woman calling for help," Jason added.

Nodding at his son, Alex said, "We had no idea what was happening, but I couldn't ignore her sounds of distress."

Melissa smiled at him like she expected nothing less, which made him feel good.

"Anyway, we approached with caution, and when I got close to Misty's house, I saw a man attacking her." He paused. "She was on the ground, begging him to leave he alone."

Her eyebrows tugging together, Melissa said, "I'm so glad you helped her."

Now that they'd gotten to know Misty and had met her husband, it gave him a different perspective. They were good people. The man that had attacked her was not. Though it pained him to have killed the man, he didn't regret it. Now the man wouldn't be able to hurt anyone else.

"What happened after you saw him attacking her?" Melissa asked.

With a glance at Jason, Alex described how he'd demanded the man get off Misty and how the man had refused, how the man had finally backed off, but when Alex had begun searching him for weapons, the man had tackled Alex.

"I managed to get on top of him, but he went for my gun," Alex said, the memory making adrenaline surge through him once again. "He even got it halfway out of my holster before I managed to gain some control. In the end though…" he clenched his jaw, "I felt I had no choice but to…to shoot him."

Melissa's eyes widened, but then she must have realized how that would come off, because a second later her face settled back to normal.

Concerned how she saw him now, he didn't say anything, giving her time to process what he'd told her.

After several long beats, she softly sighed and said, "I know you well enough to know you didn't want to have to kill either of those men, Alex. That's not who you are. But when push came to shove, you did what you had to do." Smiling softly, she added, "It helps me to know that you'll be able to do what it takes to keep us safe."

Glad she saw it that way, he leaned toward her and planted a kiss on her forehead.

"Mom! Dad!" Jason shouted. "Look out!" He leapt in front of them just as the sound of a gunshot reached Alex's ears. Then, to his horror, Alex saw red blooming on the thigh of Jason's jeans before his son collapsed to the pavement.

"He's been shot!" Melissa cried out, falling to her knees beside Jason.

As worried as Alex was for his son, his immediate reaction was to unsling his AR and point it in the direction of where the blast had come from. It took a moment, but Alex saw a man dodge behind a pillar in front of a furniture store about fifty yards away.

Why had the guy taken potshots at Alex and his group? Was it simply because he could and he feared no repercussions? Except the repercussion of Alex going after him, which he wanted to do, but when he looked at his son, he knew his son's health had to take priority over revenge.

Tamara and John rushed to join them.

"What do we do?" Melissa asked, looking to Alex for guidance.

Alex couldn't see the extent of the damage through Jason's jeans, but he knew they needed to stop the bleeding. Tearing his backpack off of his shoulders, Alex dropped to his knees beside Jason, who was moaning in pain. Frantic to help his son, he dug through the pack, coming up with the small first aid kit he'd brought along.

Opening the kit, he found several individually wrapped gauze pads, but he knew Jason would bleed through those in moments. Instead, he took off his hoodie, wadded it up, and pressed it against Jason's thigh.

"Aww! That hurts!"

"I'm sorry, son," Alex said as he pressed hard. "We've got to stop the bleeding."

With a glance at Melissa, whose face was pale as she totally focused on Jason, Alex tried to figure out what to do. Then he remembered something he'd read in a thriller. He needed to see if the bullet had gone all the way through Jason's leg or if it was still inside. But not until the bleeding had stopped.

"What if the guy shoots at us again?" Tamara asked.

Alex was wondering the same thing. He shifted his eyes to Melissa, who was looking between him and Jason. "I don't want you to get shot too," she said, her eyes filled with worry.

"I'll be careful."

With her lips pressed together like she was trying to control her emotions, she nodded and took over pressing the hoodie against Jason's leg.

"Everyone move behind that blue Nissan," Alex said, pointing to the closest car.

"What about Jason?" Melissa asked.

"I can get myself over there," he said, his face pale.

"We'll help you," Melissa said.

"We've got him," John said to Alex. "Go."

With a brisk nod, Alex shifted his attention to the pillar where he'd last seen the man who had shot his son. *Shot his son!* The thought made him furious.

Before moving from his spot, he lifted his AR and used the scope to get a closer look. Sweeping the area, he searched for any movement, but didn't see anyone. Making sure Jason, Melissa, and the others were safely behind the car, Alex blew out a breath, then crept forward.

CHAPTER 28

Alex

THERE WERE a handful of cars in the parking lot, so Alex dashed to the nearest one, all the while keeping an eye out for the shooter, who he didn't see. Scrutinizing his family's location, once he was satisfied that they were out of the line of fire, he moved to another car that was closer to the building, putting his back against the rear passenger door while keeping his head on a swivel. Inhaling two quick breaths, he dashed to the next car and the next until he was as close as he could get to the building before coming out from cover. Then he saw movement. Next to the farthest pillar.

Using the scope on his AR he searched for the shooter.

There!

The man poked his head out, seemingly unaware of Alex's proximity, his focus on Alex's group. Moving his scope down slightly, Alex searched for the man's weapon. He wanted to know what he was up against. With the man facing the pillar, only his left side was visible. His weapon obscured by his body.

Alex lifted his gun, putting the man's left shoulder and chest in his crosshairs, but the angle wasn't great, and he didn't want to risk revealing his presence. Not without a clear shot.

If he could just get closer...

Checking the area, Alex determined that the man was alone. He watched and waited, and when the man stepped behind the pillar, putting him completely out of view, which meant any movement Alex made shouldn't catch his attention, Alex sprinted to the nearest pillar, which was at the opposite end of the storefront from where the shooter was trying to conceal himself.

Pressing his back to the pillar, Alex felt his heart racing. From where he stood, when he looked to his right, he could see the car his family was crouched behind. He wondered how Jason was doing. He needed to take care of this and get back to his family, but what did *taking care of this* entail? Shooting a man in cold blood?

Like he did to Jason.

The reminder settled any reticence he may have had to do what had to be done.

He turned his head to his left where he could see through the still intact glass and into the furniture store. His reflection stared back at him. Wait. Could he see the man's reflection? No. He was too far away. Which meant the man couldn't see him either.

Alex took a quick peek around the pillar in the man's direction. The man's back was to the pillar, his eyes on the glass fronting the furniture store. Pulling back out of sight, Alex considered his next move. With another long look toward his family, who he couldn't see as they hid behind the blue car, he clenched his jaw. This was taking too long. He wanted to get Jason home—and they still had many miles to travel.

Making a decision he hoped wasn't too reckless, he swept the ground around him with his gaze until he found what he was looking for. Crouching to his right, he picked up a smallish rock, then stood and lobbed it toward a car near the shooter before getting behind the pillar again. The rock clattered against the car's hood.

That was Alex's cue.

He poked his head around the pillar on the left side this time. The shooter was looking away from Alex, his neck stretched as he tried to figure out where the noise had come from.

Taking advantage of the distraction, Alex darted to the next pillar, and then the next. Now there was only one pillar between Alex and the pillar the man was hiding behind. And now Alex could see the man's reflection in the glass.

Alex watched the man, who still seemed oblivious to Alex's presence. Instead, he was hyper-focused on the parking lot, his back to Alex.

Alex stood and tiptoed to the next pillar. Only about fifteen feet separated him from the shooter. And now if the man looked in the glass, it would be highly likely that he would see Alex. At least if Alex was standing.

Squatting, he gathered his courage, ready to be done with this. Which was when the man shifted back to where he'd been before, his eyes pointing toward the glass.

Freezing, Alex felt his heart skip a beat, his eyes locked on the shooter's reflection. The shooter's gaze was at eye level, not down where Alex was. He seemed to be attempting to use the reflection to see if anyone was sneaking up on him.

Knowing if he moved, the movement would catch the shooter's eye, Alex ran through his options, which weren't many—wait until the man looked away before moving, or go for it and chance revealing himself too soon.

Though he knew he needed to be patient, when Alex pictured Jason in pain and bleeding, his patience waned. He needed to do this. He needed to make his move.

The man glanced to his right, in Alex's direction, then to his left, then he stared forward, into the glass-fronted furniture store.

Shifting to one knee so that he could keep his balance, Alex kept his AR pointed up and pressed to his shoulder. Still hidden, Alex glanced at the shooter's reflection and confirmed that the man hadn't seemed to notice him. Yet.

Softly exhaling, Alex knew it was now or never.

Moving slowly at first, once he had his feet under him, he leapt up and swung his AR around the pillar, aiming it in the direction of the shooter. Before he had a chance to put his eye to the scope and fine tune his aim, the man turned to him with a gasp and lifted his pistol.

"Drop it!" Alex shouted as he frantically tried to get a bead on the man.

The man did as Alex demanded, which surprised Alex.

"Kick it over here."

Again, the man complied.

"Put your hands on your head."

"Don't shoot me," the man said, his eyes like saucers as he lifted his hands and placed them on his head.

"You mean like you shot my son?" Alex asked as he lifted his eyes from his scope to glare at the man.

"I wasn't aiming for him."

Narrowing his eyes, Alex said, "Who were you aiming for?"

"Uh...you?"

"What on earth for?"

The man shrugged. "I haven't eaten since yesterday morning and your group has packs. I know you have food in there."

It had been less than twenty-four hours since the EMP had hit, and already people were willing to kill for food. What would happen when more people were desperate?

"So," Alex said as he put it together, "you figured if you took me out the rest of my group would comply."

"Yeah." One side of the man's mouth tugged upward. "The kid jumped in front of you. I wasn't aiming for him."

Fury, hot and bright, surged through Alex's veins. "*But you did shoot him! You shot my son!*" Would Jason die because of this idiot?

Alex put his eye back to the scope as his finger slid toward the trigger. But when he looked at the man through his scope, saw that he was unarmed, his hands resting on his head, Alex couldn't do it. He couldn't kill an unarmed man. Half-wishing the man would pull out another gun, just to give Alex an excuse, he lifted his eye from the scope once again. "Face the pillar."

The man's face went slack. "Are you going to execute me?"

"I should."

The man licked his lips, but then he turned and faced the pillar.

"John!" Alex called out.

A moment later John's head popped up from behind the blue car.

"Come here," Alex said.

With a nod, John stood and made his way over. When he reached Alex, Alex asked, "How's Jason?"

John glanced at the man facing the pillar, then turned to Alex. "He's okay. The bleeding stopped, and when we opened up his pant leg...well, it looks like it's just a flesh wound."

Relief, pure and sweet, replaced the fury that had been roaring inside Alex. "Can you search him?" Alex asked with a head nod in the shooter's direction.

"Yeah."

Alex and John approached the man, stopping beside him. "Don't move," Alex commanded.

The man nodded, and as John did a thorough pat-down, Alex kept his AR trained on the shooter.

John turned to Alex and shook his head, then he picked up the man's gun and held it at his side.

Alex focused on the shooter. "I'm going to let you live." Hoping he wasn't making a mistake but knowing it would be impossible to live with himself if he shot an unarmed man, he added, "Don't make me regret it."

The man turned his head and met Alex's gaze. "You won't." He paused. "Thank you for not..." he swallowed hard. "For not killing me."

Huffing out a breath, Alex shook his head and frowned. "Beat it."

The man nodded, then turned and ran off, heading north. Alex watched him go until he was out of sight, then he turned to John. "Did I do the right thing? Letting him go?"

"What else could you have done? Turned him in to the police? How would you do that? So then, what? Shoot him? In cold blood?" His lips twisted as he shook his head. "That wouldn't be right."

Feeling better about his decision, Alex let a small smile curve his lips. "That was my thinking too. Now, let me see how my son is doing."

CHAPTER 29

Melissa

THE ENTIRE TIME Alex had been going after the shooter, Melissa's stomach had been churning. But when he called John over, she felt some relief. He wouldn't have called him over if things weren't under control, right?

"What's happening?" Jason asked, the color in his cheeks better than it had been earlier as he sat on the asphalt, his back against the car.

"I don't know." Moving until she was squatting on the balls of her feet, she rose until she was able to see through the windows on the car they were hiding behind. Alex and John were a distance away—past the sidewalk and on the other side of the parking lot—but she was still able to see a man with his hands on his head facing a white pillar. Alex was holding his rifle on the man and John was talking to Alex. A few moments later, Alex said something to the man and he ran off.

Why had Alex let him go?

Then she reminded herself that these weren't normal times. It wasn't like they could call the police and have them pick the man up. And she wasn't surprised that Alex hadn't shot him when he'd disarmed him. She only hoped the man would crawl back into the hole he'd come out of and not bother them—or anyone else—anymore.

When she saw Alex and John walking toward them, she stood. "Looks like we can go." She turned to Jason. "How are you feeling? Are you going to be able to walk?"

He grimaced a bit but nodded. "I kind of have to, don't I?"

Wishing she could call an ambulance to come help her son, a new worry filled her mind. Even if his injury was only a flesh wound, what about infection? They needed to get their hands on antibiotics.

"What happened?" Melissa asked Alex when he and John joined them.

Alex gave a brief replay of his conversation with the man, then frowned. "I couldn't shoot an unarmed man."

Melissa smiled at him and placed a hand on his arm. "No. Of course not."

Alex knelt beside Jason. "Let me see the wound."

Jason nodded, and Alex lifted the wadded-up hoodie from Jason's thigh, examining the area where the bullet had torn out a small chunk of flesh. A muscle moved in Alex's jaw as he shook his head. "John, can you hand me a couple of gauze pads from the first aid kit?"

"Yep," he said as he removed a few items from the first aid

kit. "We wanted you to take a look at the wound before we covered it."

With a nod, Alex ripped open the packaging, then gently placed a large square of sterile gauze over the wound. Thankfully the bleeding had slowed. After the gauze was in place, Alex wrapped an Ace bandage around Jason's leg, securing the gauze more firmly.

"We need to find antibiotics," Melissa said, her earlier thought filling her mind.

Alex looked at her, his lips twisting into a frown. "You're right. But first we need to get home." He paused. "We'll keep an eye out for a pharmacy on the way."

That sounded like a good plan to Melissa. "Okay." Worried about how Jason was going to do for the long walk, she bit her lip as she watched him.

He smiled up at her. "I'll be okay, Mom."

Grateful his injury wasn't more severe, she smiled back, although she wasn't sure how well he would actually be able to walk.

He pushed himself to his feet, and after standing there for a few moments, said, "All right. I'm ready."

They began walking, but after being shot at twice now, the first time being the day before when three of her group had been killed, Melissa couldn't stop her anxiety from ratcheting up. It felt as if bullets could come flying toward them at any moment, injuring, or even killing, any one of them.

This was no way to live.

CHRISTINE KERSEY

She was desperate to get home where she would feel relatively safe.

Jason hobbled along, doing better than Melissa had expected. Then again, he'd never been one to complain, so for all Melissa knew, he was in all kinds of pain and just not saying anything about it.

Soon, they reached the I-215 overpass. As they crossed it, Melissa looked toward the road below, a six-lane Interstate highway. Abandoned cars were stopped here and there. A few were piled up.

"What's that?" Tamara asked, pointing off to the west.

Melissa squinted in the direction she was pointing to, but it wasn't hard to see the thick column of smoke that filled the sky. "Must be a fire."

"Could be from a downed plane," John said.

Melissa spun around and looked at him. "A downed plane?"

He nodded. "Yeah. When the EMP struck, the planes would have lost all of their power and crashed."

Horrified by the idea, Melissa realized she hadn't even thought about that. What other terrible things had happened that she hadn't considered?

"Why didn't we see any planes crash?" Jason asked as he leaned against the railing that overlooked I-215 like he was trying to take the weight off of his injured leg.

Melissa bit her lip, worried for her son but not able to do anything to help him.

"The flight path is on the west side of the valley," John said in answer to Jason's question. "Not over here."

"Oh," Jason said with a nod. "Right."

Melissa didn't want to think about how terrifying it would have been to be on one of those flights, and she definitely didn't want to consider how many lives had been lost the day before just from plane crashes.

"Do you think the EMP affected the entire country?" Tamara asked.

They all looked at each other, but no one knew the answer.

"I wouldn't be surprised," Alex finally said. "I mean, if it was done maliciously by one of the countries that hate us, then yeah, I would expect they'd make sure the whole country was hit." He grimaced. "And I suspect it was done maliciously."

Wondering what else their attacker had in store for them, Melissa said, "Let's keep going." Where they stood was way too exposed.

They trudged forward, and after they'd gone another half mile, Jason pointed and said, "Hey, isn't that our truck?"

CHAPTER 30

Alex

Peering in the direction Jason pointed, when Alex recognized the truck they'd acquired the day before, but which had then been stolen from them, he laughed. "Yeah. It is." Fresh enthusiasm rushed through him. They wouldn't have to walk the rest of the way home, which would certainly be good for Jason. At least he hoped that's how things would go. He didn't know what shape the truck was in or if it had any fuel left. It was about a hundred yards ahead, parked haphazardly in the middle of the road like whoever had been driving it had randomly stopped and jumped out, abandoning it.

Wait. What if the thieves were still in the area?

Scanning the general vicinity, he saw a medical office building nearby. Were the thieves inside? Was that why they'd stopped? How many were there?

"Hold up," he said, his voice only loud enough for his

group to hear. "We don't know if whoever took it is still around. We need to approach with caution."

All five of them had stopped.

"Maybe they have antibiotics in one of those medical offices," Melissa said.

That was a good point. But would it be better to look for medication now or to jump in the truck and get the heck out of there? Alex turned to Jason, whose face was pale. "How are you doing?"

A tentative smile tugged at Jason's lips, but it seemed forced. "Okay."

Alex looked at Jason's leg, but the blood on his jeans from the initial injury obscured his ability to see if it had started bleeding again. Kneeling in front of his son, he pulled back the torn denim. He immediately saw that blood was seeping through the ACE bandage. He got to his feet, his decision made. "We'll take the truck and look for antibiotics somewhere else."

Everyone nodded.

Now they just needed to get to the truck and drive away before the thieves noticed.

Only a few cars sat between them and the truck. Thinking about it for a moment, Alex said, "Let's just walk toward it, but don't act interested in it. Once we get close, we need to be subtle in checking to see if anyone's around."

Once everyone agreed, they began walking. Alex noticed that Jason's limp was becoming more pronounced. He imagined having a chunk of flesh torn out by a bullet would be painful. Admiration for his son's stoicism washed over Alex. Jason was only seventeen, but his maturity and ability to deal with adversity was impressive. It also gave Alex hope. Because there was no doubt that they were only at the very beginning of all the adversity they had yet to face, and Alex and Melissa would need their son's strength and courage to help their family get through this.

"I don't see anyone around," Melissa murmured from beside him.

Thirty feet separated them from the truck. Alex glanced to his right where houses lined one side of the four-lane road, then to his left toward the medical complex. He didn't see anyone either.

It didn't take long to close the distance between them and the truck.

"Everyone get down on this side of the truck," Alex said, motioning to the pavement beside the passenger side, which faced away from the medical complex. He figured if the thieves were anywhere, it would be in there and he would prefer not to be seen until there was no other option.

Once he was satisfied his group was sufficiently concealed, he opened the passenger door, and kneeling on the ground, he peered inside. His gaze went to the steering column. Just as he'd figured, whoever had stolen the truck had hot-wired it and now there was nowhere to insert the key.

Although he'd never hot-wired a car, Alex was an engineer and usually able to figure things out. Only difference was, this time he had to hurry. Lives were on the line. The lives of his wife and son, not to mention John and Tamara.

He crawled inside the truck, and laying across the bench seat, he examined the exposed wires. A group of wires were twisted together, and a separate wire was near the group but not touching it. Alex only had a rudimentary idea of how cars were hot-wired, but he did know that one wire had to be touched to another. Keeping an eye on the medical building, he moved to the driver's seat, pressed the clutch in, then carefully took hold of the protective casing around the single wire before touching it against the bundle of wires. To his surprise and delight, the car's engine started right up. He removed the starter wire from the bundle and the engine stayed on. Bending the starter wire away from the bundle, he made sure the emergency brake was on, put the truck in neutral, and slid back out of the truck on the passenger side.

"I think someone's coming," Melissa urgently whispered.

Panic swept over him. "Jason, you and John get in the bed of the truck and lay down. Melissa and Tamara follow me into the cab." Not waiting to make sure everyone understood, Alex launched himself into the truck through the passenger side and scrambled to get behind the steering wheel.

"Hey!" a man shouted from the medical complex. "Hey! What do you think you're doing? Get out of my truck!"

Waiting long enough for Tamara and Melissa to get in and close the door, once Alex made sure John and Jason were in the bed of the truck, he put the truck into gear and let off the clutch as he accelerated. The truck lurched forward.

Two men were running after them, but they were about fifty yards behind the truck. Lifting his gaze to the rearview mirror, Alex saw both men pointing pistols in their direction. "Everyone down!"

Melissa and Tamara leaned forward, hugging their knees. John and Jason were already lying down in the bed of the truck. Multiple gunshots rang out, but it didn't sound like any bullets hit the truck. Although Alex wanted to duck too, he forced himself to stay upright and in control of the truck.

It didn't take long to be out of range of the men's guns and for them to disappear from sight.

Breathing a sigh of relief, Alex smiled at Melissa, who sat next to the passenger window with Tamara sitting between them on the bench seat. He would have preferred to have Melissa next to him, but he guessed she was probably more comfortable with guns than her friend, so it made sense to have her riding shotgun.

He silently smiled, understanding more than ever the meaning of that term.

"I can't believe we got this truck back," Melissa said with a grin.

"Just in time too," Alex said with a chin lift to the snowflakes that had begun floating down and settling on the windshield before melting away. And thankfully, the windows were all intact.

CHAPTER 31

Melissa

Melissa looked over her shoulder at Jason and John in the bed of the truck. They must be freezing back there. Maybe they could all squeeze into the cab, but when she looked at how little space there was, she knew that wasn't possible.

"If you turn left here," Tamara said, "my house isn't too much farther."

Melissa had almost forgotten that they would be dropping off Tamara and John. Jason could join her and Alex in the cab then.

When Alex turned left, Melissa found herself closely scrutinizing the area, on the lookout for anyone who might wish to harm them. Not a lot of people were out, probably due to the cold and snowfall. There wasn't enough snow to stick to the road, but it certainly was enough to cause a chill. "Does the heater work in here?"

Alex fiddled with the knobs. "I don't think it does."

Shivering, Melissa was still grateful to be riding in the truck, which was preferable to being on foot.

"Turn right here," Tamara said.

After a few more turns, they arrived at Tamara's house and Alex pulled into her driveway.

"Do you want me to come in with you?" Alex offered. "To make sure everything is okay inside?"

"Yes," she said, then she turned to Melissa. "You can all come in if you want."

Eager to get home to her other children, she shook her head. "I want to get going as soon as we can."

Alex put the truck in neutral to keep the engine running and turned to Melissa. "I'll leave it idling. I shouldn't be long."

Nodding, Melissa opened her door and got out, and after Tamara climbed out as well, Melissa gave her a hug. "Take care."

Nodding, Tamara smiled. "You too."

While Alex accompanied Tamara inside, Melissa spoke to Jason and John who were now sitting up in the bed of the truck. "We'll be dropping John off soon, so Jason, why don't you get in the cab with Dad and me?"

He visibly shivered, then nodded. "I think I will."

"Are you doing okay back here, John?" Melissa asked as Jason climbed over the side of the truck, wincing as he did.

John chuckled. "I have to admit that I've been better, but I sure do appreciate having a ride."

Alex joined them a few minutes later. "Tamara's husband and daughter made it home."

Happy that Tamara had been reunited with her family, she smiled. "That's great."

"I gave them our address," Alex added. "Just in case." He handed a slip of paper to John. "I wrote it down for you too."

John pocketed the piece of paper. "Thank you. I really appreciate all you and Melissa have done for me."

Melissa tilted her head. "What did I do for you?"

He chuckled. "I know some of the others in our group thought I would slow everyone down, but Tamara told me you spoke up for me."

It had only been the day before, but yeah, Melissa remembered how Dillon, who was now dead, had been annoyed that John would be coming with them. "I'm glad you were with us."

"Thanks," John said with a smile, then he gave Alex directions to his house.

After that, Melissa climbed into the cab, sitting in the middle. Jason got in after her, taking the spot beside the passenger window. When Alex opened the driver's door to get in, Melissa noticed a large red stain on the seat. Pointing to it, she asked, "Is that..." She wrinkled her nose. "Blood?"

"Uh-huh," Alex said as he got behind the wheel.

Realizing how truly dangerous the men they'd taken the truck back from actually were and how lucky they'd been to get away with the truck, she felt a combination of fear and great relief.

"It's from the guy Dad shot," Jason said from beside her.

Her eyebrows shot up and she turned to Jason before shifting her attention to Alex. "What?"

Rather than look her way, he kept his eyes pointed to the road. "We already talked about this."

"I know. I just...I thought it was from the men who took the truck. That they'd...well, killed someone." But nope. It was her own husband who was the dangerous one. Only in his case he'd been protecting their family.

Would she have been able to do the same thing if it had been up to her? Kill someone to protect her children? Yes, in fact, she had no doubt she would be able to do whatever it took to protect her children. Which settled any misgivings she had about what Alex had done.

A few minutes later they reached John's house. She and Alex got out of the truck to tell John goodbye, and after he went into his house, they got back in the truck and drove out of the neighborhood, turning south on 1300 East.

"How long do you think it will take to get home?" Jason asked, which reminded Melissa that her son was injured, almost certainly in pain, and in need of antibiotics.

"We're about five miles away," Alex said, which didn't seem like much now that they were in a vehicle. "But since we have to go kind of slow to get around the stalled vehicles, it'll probably take at least twenty minutes."

Melissa couldn't believe they would be home so soon. Ecstatic, she forced herself to rein in her enthusiasm. Anything could happen between here and home.

CHAPTER 32

Alex

Swerving around a white SUV, Alex was on high alert. In this stretch of road there were two lanes in each direction with a wide concrete median dividing them. In addition, a concrete wall—a sound barrier for the houses that backed up to this street—lined both sides of the road. In other words, if some obstruction appeared, or if someone tried to attack them, they would have no way to escape, nowhere to go.

Tension grew inside him. They needed to get through this section of road as quickly as possible, but that was difficult with all the stalled cars. And when he saw a pair of cars up ahead stalled so close together that there was no way around, he audibly sighed.

"Can you drive over the median?" Melissa asked.

Small bushes and trees were in the median, which would

make it a challenge to drive over. Still, what choice did he have?

"Guess we'll have to," he said. Looking for a spot where the bushes were lower, he eased the steering wheel to the left, downshifted, and goosed the gas pedal. The left front tire bumped up onto the concrete curb of the median. The right front tire quickly followed. Not sure how well the old truck would handle jumping the curb, he went for it, bouncing over the island and thumping down onto the other side.

"That was fun," Jason said with a lopsided grin.

Alex burst out laughing, which released some of the tension he'd been holding in his chest. It felt great. "Yeah, it kind of was, wasn't it?"

Melissa was smiling as well.

Not too far ahead, Alex could see that on the right side of the road, the concrete wall ended and a shopping center began. Just before that though was a turnoff to a neighborhood. On the left side of the road, however, the side they were currently on, the wall continued beyond his view. Wanting to be on the side where escape would be possible, once they passed the stalled cars that had been blocking the road, he said, "Hold on, guys. I'm going back over the median." Then he made his way across. The truck protested more this time, but with encouragement from gunning it, the truck made it over.

The end of the wall wasn't too far now.

Almost there, he thought, his attention focused on driving around an inoperative compact car.

Then, from the turnoff to the neighborhood on the right, a woman came running into the road, waving her hands and yelling something Alex couldn't make out.

"Watch out!" Melissa shouted.

Not sure if her comment was directed at him or the woman who was now directly in their path, Alex had no choice but to slam on the brakes, because he wasn't about to mow down a woman in the street.

The woman, who looked like she was in her late fifties, wore jeans and a jacket. She didn't appear to be armed, and at the look of complete distress on her face, Alex didn't think she meant them harm. Instead, she seemed desperate to get help, her arms curling over her head and her eyes frantic as she approached the truck.

Alex used the hand crank to roll down the window, the truck idling.

"Please," the woman said as she ran her fingers through her hair, her stare pained. "My husband needs help."

Not about to follow blindly, Alex asked, "What's wrong with him?"

"It's his heart. He's..." She bit her lip and shook her head. "He's having chest pains."

As awful as that was, Alex didn't know what he could do for him.

"Please," the woman said as tears slid down her cheeks.

"We can at least go see," Melissa murmured from beside him.

Suppressing a sigh, Alex nodded, then said to the woman, "Lead the way."

The woman pressed a palm to her heart. "Thank you." Then she turned and began trotting back toward the neighborhood.

"You sure you want to follow her?" Alex asked Melissa. "It will delay us getting to Emily and Steven."

Melissa nodded. "It shouldn't take too long. Besides, after all the bad that's happened," she glanced at the dark stain on the seat next to her, "it would be nice to do something positive for a change."

He couldn't argue with that. He looked up, saw the woman had paused at the entrance to the neighborhood, and turned the steering wheel in her direction as he accelerated. A few moments later they pulled in front of a modest house.

"Stay here," Alex told Melissa and Jason. He wanted to keep the truck running so they could take off as soon as possible. Plus, if there was trouble, he wanted his family to be able to get away. After putting the truck in neutral, he got out and followed the woman inside. A man was stretched out on the couch, his eyes closed. Was he still alive?

The woman knelt beside the man. "Darren, I brought help."

The man's eyes fluttered open. "Margaret?"

Okay, he was still alive. Still, Alex didn't know what the woman expected him to do. Then a thought occurred to him. "Why didn't you ask your neighbors for help? I mean, why me?"

Her eyebrows jumped together and she shook her head like the answer was obvious. "He needs to go to the hospital, but none of their cars work."

Oh. Now it made sense.

"You'll take him, right?" she asked, her eyes shiny with concern.

There was a hospital not far down the road, and it was right on the way home, so he nodded. "Yeah. I can drop him off."

She leapt to her feet as a beaming smile lit her face. "Thank you!" She fell to the carpet beside her husband. "See? I knew help would come."

Her husband barely managed a nod.

"Let's get you to their truck," she said, then she looked to Alex for help.

Between him and the woman—Margaret—they managed to get Darren out the door and to the truck. Jason opened the passenger door and got out, and though he was struggling himself, he said, "I'll get in back."

Alex helped Darren get into the passenger seat.

The snow had slowed to an occasional flake, although it was still cold.

Jason and Margaret got into the bed of the truck and Alex got behind the wheel. As they got back on 1300 East, it occurred to him that while they were at the hospital they should see if they could get help for Jason. Surely there were doctors still working.

It was slow going, but eventually they made it to the

hospital. Alex pulled right up to the doors of the Emergency Room entrance. Although there were no other working vehicles that he could see, there were plenty of people around, which made him nervous. Would someone try to steal their truck, their only means of transportation? Wanting to drop Darren and Margaret off and leave, when he glanced in the rearview mirror and saw Jason sitting in the truck bed looking toward the entrance, he knew the most important thing was to get his son medical care.

"Maybe they can help Jason," Melissa said as if she'd read his mind.

"Yeah," he said with a nod. "We'll take him inside and see."

With the truck idling, Alex got out and spoke to Margaret. "Why don't you see if you can get a wheelchair?"

She nodded, climbed out of the truck's bed, and disappeared inside the hospital. A few moments later, she came out, pushing a wheelchair. Glad she'd found one, Alex helped Darren into the chair.

"Thank you so much," Margaret said with tears in her eyes.

Feeling good about something he'd done for a change, Alex nodded. "Good luck to you."

She smiled, then began pushing the man inside.

Alex got back in the truck.

"Aren't we going to take Jason inside?"

"Yes, but let's park first."

Ignoring the stares of the few people in the area, Alex

drove the truck into the parking lot, then he popped the clutch, which killed the engine.

Melissa turned to him with wide eyes as her mouth fell open. "How are we going to drive the truck home now?"

Giving her a lopsided smile, he said, "Popping the clutch was the simplest way to turn off the engine. I should be able to start it again with the wires like I did before."

"Okay. If you're sure."

He laughed. "I am. Once we're home, I'll see about fixing the ignition so we can use the key again." He leaned forward and met Jason's gaze. "Now, let's get you taken care of and get home."

"Sounds good to me," he said.

Once they were all out of the truck, Jason used his keys to lock the doors—he didn't want to give someone else the opportunity to take the truck and hoped they wouldn't be inside long enough for someone to try. Then the three of them trooped inside. Every chair was taken, so injured and sick people were sitting on the floor with their backs against the wall or lying on the ground, moaning and bleeding. The couple they'd brought to the hospital was talking to a woman who looked like she worked at the hospital. Well, Margaret was talking, Darren was slumped forward in the wheelchair.

"Maybe we should just go, Dad," Jason said from beside him.

Scanning the space and seeing nowhere to sit but the floor, and with others looking a lot worse off than they were,

Alex frowned. "Let me see if I can at least get some antibiotics."

"Maybe we should wait in the truck," Melissa said.

"Hold on a sec. They might need to see Jason before they give me any meds."

She nodded. "All right."

He left them near the door and went in search of someone to assist him, but no one was around except the person Margaret was talking to. He went over and stood behind them.

"Sir," the woman talking to the couple said to him, "please back up."

Margaret spun around and looked at Alex, but when she saw him standing behind her, relief filled her eyes like she thought he was there to help her. She turned back to the worker. "It's okay. He's with us."

The worker nodded and said, "Like I said, ma'am, we'll get to your husband as soon as we can."

Margaret swiveled her head to Alex. "They're too busy to see him right away."

Surprised, because Darren seemed to be in pretty bad shape, Alex suppressed a sigh and said, "If you don't see him immediately, he's going to die."

Margaret gave him a pained look, like she didn't want to believe that, but then she nodded.

The worker audibly sighed. "I'll do what I can." She turned to leave, but Alex said, "Wait." She stopped and looked at him, exasperation clear on her face.

"My son, he was shot. It's just a flesh wound, but I was wondering if we could get some antibiotics."

She pinched the bridge of her nose and closed her eyes, then met his gaze. "The doctor will have to take care of that. Please fill out a paper form and we'll get to him when we can." Without waiting for him to argue, she turned and strode away.

Alex turned and looked at the mass of people waiting to be seen, and knowing that even Darren wasn't a high priority, he had little hope that Jason would be seen anytime that day. Deciding not to get upset—he knew it wasn't the fault of any of the hospital employees that the world had come crashing down—he looked at Margaret and frowned, then shook his head.

Her shoulders slumped like she felt defeated. Having an idea how she felt, although he was confident Jason would survive—he had to!—he placed a hand of comfort on her arm, then turned and walked back to Melissa and Jason.

"Well?" Melissa asked, her forehead creased.

"We can wait for hours and hours to maybe be seen and maybe get antibiotics, or we can go home, check on the kids, and then go search for some on our own."

Melissa shifted her eyes to Jason, who grinned and said, "Option two. Definitely."

CHAPTER 33

Melissa

Though disappointed they couldn't immediately get antibiotics for Jason, Melissa was eager to get home and make sure Emily and Steven were all right. Walking beside Alex and Jason, when she saw that the truck was right where they'd left it, she felt a knot of worry in her gut uncoil. She hadn't even realized how much she'd feared that they would come out and the truck would be gone. Of course, they hadn't been inside long, but people had seen them drive the truck in, and with not many vehicles working, she was certain there were plenty of people who would be happy to take one of the rare working vehicles. Of course, the reason they even had it didn't sit all that well with her, but what had happened was in the past so there was no point in feeling guilty about it. The world had changed and she was already changing right along with it.

Alex unlocked the passenger door and helped her and

Jason in, then he went around the hood to his side and climbed in as well. Melissa watched him touch the wires together and heard the engine start up.

"Let's go home," Alex said, which sounded like the best idea Melissa had ever heard.

As they drove out of the parking lot and got back onto 1300 East, Melissa found herself leaning forward as if that would make them go faster. Forcing herself to relax, she straightened against the bench seat and watched Alex maneuver around one inoperative vehicle after another. But they were on another stretch of road like the one where Margaret had flagged them down—with sound barrier walls on both sides of the road and a plant-filled median dividing the four lanes of traffic.

With the way Alex was frowning intently and with his hands gripping the steering wheel, she began to feel a quiver in her stomach from the rising tension. Was someone else going to jump out in front of them? Would it be someone who wanted to help themselves to the truck rather than someone who needed help?

Kind of desperate to make the fear go away, she touched Alex's knee and said, "We're almost home. I'm sure we'll get there without any trouble."

He gave her a sharp look, like she was daring fate.

"Don't jinx it, Mom," Jason said, his face totally serious.

Had she?

Softly exhaling, she kept her gaze riveted to the road ahead.

They passed the library and the concrete wall disappeared, replaced by an open field.

Half a mile on, Alex abruptly angled into the left turn lane and began turning into a parking lot.

Alarmed, Melissa asked, "What are you doing?"

"Stopping at the grocery store. They have a pharmacy inside. Maybe we can get some antibiotics."

Swallowing over her trepidation, she nodded. The sooner Jason started on the medication, the better chance he had of avoiding an infection, something that could become very serious in the world they now lived in. And she knew that the precious commodity would only become harder to find the longer they waited. Despite her misgivings, this was a necessary stop. "Okay," she said. "Are we all going in?"

"I'll stay in the truck," Jason said, wincing a bit as he spoke. "To guard it."

Not liking leaving him on his own, she could see he wasn't in the best shape to go into the store. What if they had to make a run for it? He would struggle to keep up.

"Good idea, son," Alex said. "Your mother and I will go in."

"Shouldn't I stay with him?"

Alex shook his head. "We need to stock up on first aid supplies while we're in there. Just in case."

Just in case someone else in their family got shot? Is that what he meant? But she knew it was more than that, although getting shot was also a distinct possibility. Any number of injuries could occur. Injuries that used to be minor, but in this world of limited medical help could quickly become major.

Not loving the idea of leaving Jason on his own, she agreed.

Alex drove the truck, which seemed extra loud at that moment, drawing the attention of the other shoppers—more like looters, but who was she to judge?—into a parking space. He popped the clutch, killing the engine. There were half a dozen parking spaces between them and the store entrance, two with cars parked in them. Dead cars, she was sure. They looked too new to be running.

Holding back a chuckle at the incongruity of the thought, when Alex handed his AR to Jason, her humor evaporated. "Why are you giving him that?"

Alex's lips flattened. "To ward off any would-be car thieves."

With each passing second, Melissa was liking this plan less and less. She turned to Jason with a stern look. "We can replace this truck. We can't replace you. If it's your life or this truck, give them the truck." Hoping for Alex's agreement, she turned to him with raised eyebrows.

He nodded. "Absolutely."

Wearing a determined look, Jason nodded. "Okay."

Alex opened his door and held it for Melissa, who slid across the blood-stained driver's seat and jumped to the pavement. Alex took his backpack out of the bed of the truck, removed a flashlight, then tossed the backpack onto the seat.

"Keep the doors locked," he said to Jason before pressing the lock on his door and closing it.

The chill in the air hadn't abated at all, and the dark gray clouds threatened more snow. Shivering, and not just from the cold, when Alex took her hand, Melissa felt slightly better, although as she watched people shoving past each other at the entrance to the store, she was reminded of her unpleasant experience the day before when she'd gotten her sneakers. Good thing Tyler had stepped in to help her. Poor Tyler.

Biting her lip to keep the sudden pressure of tears at bay, she walked beside Alex toward the store entrance. There were two sets of glass doors. One set had been pried open, but the other set had been shattered. Most people were squeezing through the pried-open doors, but some didn't want to wait and ducked below the crossbar on the shattered door, ignoring the shards of glass that clung to the door frame.

"Hurry up!" a woman shouted to a man trying to shove his large body through the narrow opening of the pried-open doors.

The man stopped and glared at her. She clamped her lips shut as she backed up a few steps. The man took his time pushing inside. Melissa stood beside Alex and waited. There was no rushing this guy and she didn't want to chance catching on the glass shards.

Finally, he was through. The woman followed, and when she was in, she gave the man a wide berth.

Alex went through first, and when he was inside the store, he motioned for Melissa to follow. With a glance at the truck and Jason, she moved to the narrow gap but easily slid between the partially opened doors.

Once inside, she had to blink a few times. Although it wasn't all that sunny outside, it was much dimmer inside the store. Alex took her hand, and they went deeper into the interior, pausing to see where the pharmacy was located.

"There it is," Melissa said a few moments later. Together, they hurried in that direction, bypassing other shopper-looters.

In the distance, a man shouted and a woman screamed obscenities. Down a nearby aisle, a man shoved a woman to the floor and took the box of cereal she'd been cradling against her chest.

"Hey!" The woman shouted, getting to her feet. "Hey! That's mine!" She took chase after him, running right past Melissa and Alex and throwing herself at the man's back. He shook her off and walked toward the exit.

"Must be his favorite cereal," Alex murmured, which nearly made Melissa choke on a much-needed burst of laughter.

The woman leapt to her feet and ran after the man in hot pursuit.

Shaking her head at the craziness of it, Melissa could only imagine how bad things would get once food was gone.

They reached the pharmacy, but when Melissa saw that the metal sliding doors at the windows were severely bent but still in place, she shifted her attention to the door that led into the back. Wide open, it hung on its hinges as if someone had forced their way in.

With all the commotion around them, her chest tightened with a sense of urgency to get what they needed and get out. It felt like severe violence could erupt at any moment. Swallowing over a knot of trepidation, she looked at Alex.

With pursed lips, he met her gaze. "Let's see what's left."

"Shouldn't I see what other supplies I can get?"

Clenching his jaw, he shook his head. "Let's stay together."

That sounded good to her, and she walked beside him toward the back area. When they reached the door, they paused. A man was inside, gripping a small flashlight in his teeth as he frantically pawed through what medication was on the shelves. He seemed harmless enough, so when Alex turned on his flashlight and shone it inside, Melissa walked into the room with Alex right behind her.

"What are you looking for?" she asked the man.

He barely glanced at them, his focus on searching the shelves, but then he removed the flashlight from between his lips. "Flovent. My wife has asthma and is about to run out of her meds."

Melissa hadn't thought about all the people with chronic illnesses who would need their medication. Wanting to help him, she said, "We're looking for antibiotics, but if I see any Flovent I'll let you know."

The man tossed her a smile. "Thank you." Then he jammed the flashlight into his mouth and continued searching.

Alex was already rummaging through the shelves.

"Let me hold the flashlight," she said to him.

He handed it to her, and she pointed it at the shelf he was searching through. Now he could use two hands.

"Found it!" The man shouted in triumph, the flashlight in one hand and several boxes in the other. He turned and ran out of the room.

Shaking her head, Melissa sighed. "What are we looking for exactly? Amoxicillin? What else?"

Alex shrugged. "I remember using Cipro one time. And isn't there one called something like Azithromycin? Those are the only ones I know."

Feeling kind of helpless, all Melissa could do was agree.

"I think this is it!" he said a few minutes later as he examined a bottle in his hand. "Amoxicillin."

Relieved, she watched as he tucked the bottle into a back pocket. "Now let's see if there are other first aid supplies we can get."

A few moments later they stood in front of the shelves were first-aid supplies were sold. There wasn't a lot left, but they managed to get a few bandages and antibiotic creams.

"This will have to do," Alex said.

Glad they'd been able to at least get some things, Melissa nodded agreement. They carried their items to the register area just so they could put them in a bag. A few other people had the same idea as they shoved the food they'd put in their carts into bags.

A gunshot rang out. Startled, when Melissa realized the sound had come from outside, she turned to Alex. "Jason!"

Alex's eyes flared, then with the bag of their supplies in one hand, he used his other to take Melissa's hand before running toward the doors.

CHAPTER 34

Alex

When they reached the exit, there was a bottleneck several people deep. Looking toward the parking lot, Alex saw a small group of people gathered beside the truck but he couldn't see if Jason was still inside or what exactly was happening.

"Get out of the way!" he shouted at the people blocking the exit.

"Wait your turn," a man grumbled from ahead of him.

Frantic to get to his son, Alex pulled out his gun and shot it into the air.

People screamed and covered their heads as debris fell from the ceiling.

"Move!" he demanded. "Now!"

The people parted like a miracle, and after he and Melissa

reached the door, he ushered her through, then quickly followed. Once outside, they raced toward the truck as light snow filtered to the ground.

Two men and a woman were bunched up by the driver's side, but the doors were still closed. Alex strained to see Jason as he hurried toward the truck. Where was he? And had that gunshot come from here? Had Jason been the one shooting? Or had someone shot at him? The windows were still intact, so it seemed unlikely that any bullets had flown.

"What's going on?" Alex shouted as he reached the truck and handed Melissa the bag that held the antibiotics and first aid supplies.

"It's a working truck," a man with a dark beard said to him, "and there's a kid inside that won't let anyone in."

Alex was close enough now that he could see inside. There was Jason, the AR in his hands pointed toward the people just outside the door. He looked unharmed. Relief surged through Alex's veins.

Pretending like he was just an interested bystander, he faced Dark Beard. "How do you know it's working?"

"Gotta be," he said. "It's an older truck and only older vehicles seem to work. Plus, why would the kid be inside if it don't work?"

Alex appraised the man. He looked like he was in his thirties and in decent shape. The other man looked older, maybe in his early sixties, and was overweight. The woman stood quietly beside the older man. Alex guessed they were together. Maybe all three were together.

"Has anyone tried to get in?" Alex asked.

Dark Beard swung an arm toward the truck. "The kid's armed with an AR, so no."

Suppressing a grin, Alex felt pride wash over him. Alex was holding his ground.

With Melissa behind him, Alex backed up a few steps, putting a several feet between himself and the group. "That's my son in there and this is my truck. I'd appreciate it if you would all give us some space."

"What?" Dark Beard said, his face scrunched up as a vein visibly pulsed in his neck.

Not wanting a confrontation, especially when he had no idea if these people were armed, Alex kept a close eye on the trio. He also kept his hand near his gun, ready to draw on anyone who appeared threatening.

Wearing a look of disgust, Dark Beard, who seemed to be speaking for everyone, shook his head and huffed a sigh.

When no one moved back, Alex felt the tension in his body rise. "Step back," he commanded.

Dark Beard crossed his arms over his chest. "Now, why should I do that?"

Getting angry, Alex tilted his head and narrowed his eyes. "If my son wasn't armed, what were you going to do? Steal my truck?" He pushed aside the memory of how he'd gotten the truck. That was irrelevant now. For all intents and purposes, the truck now belonged to him.

The question seemed to catch the man off guard, like he

hadn't quite thought it through. Or maybe didn't want to admit flat-out that he was ready to steal from a kid.

"Come on, son," the older man said as he placed a hand on Dark Beard's arm. "Let's go home."

Dark Beard made a scoffing sound, then spit on the ground near Alex's feet. Ignoring that, Alex stood there, waiting to see if the man would leave. Finally, after several tense moments, Dark Beard frowned deeply and shook his head, then turned and stormed away. The other two followed.

When all three people were a distance away, Alex turned to Jason, giving him a nod. A moment later his son unlocked the door. Alex helped Melissa inside, climbed in beside her, then closed and locked his door. He pushed in the clutch and tapped the wires together, and after the truck started, he put the truck in neutral while he bent the wires away from each other. Then he put the truck in gear and drove away from the store.

"What happened?" he asked once they were back on 1300 East and heading toward home. "We heard a gunshot."

"I don't know. It wasn't from me, and it wasn't those guys." He paused. "They just, they showed up and started yelling at me to get out and give them the truck." He shook his head. "I wasn't about to just hand it over. I mean, what the heck? So I pointed the AR at them and they stopped yelling at me and then you got there."

Glad they'd arrived before things had escalated, Alex found himself clenching his teeth. Society had collapsed at lightning speed. But when he thought about it, throughout the world's history society had often been on the brink, and more often than not, over the brink. Just because all he'd known was a life where law and order ruled and citizens had a clear idea of what to expect day to day didn't mean that was normal to humankind. Nope. What was happening now—every person for themselves, kill or be killed, do whatever you had to do to survive—*that*, unfortunately, was the natural way of things, the base nature of mankind. And really, it was how many places in the world had been living well before the EMP had shattered Alex's way of life. It was just new to him. And he hated it. Even so, it was the new normal and he would have to adjust. Had already started to adjust.

Working to relax his mind and body, he thought about the reason they'd stopped at the store in the first place. Glancing at Jason, he said, "We got antibiotics."

Jason smiled. "That's great."

Alex steered around a black SUV that was partially blocking the right lane and was halfway onto the sidewalk. It looked as if the driver had lost control when the EMP had killed the electronics in the vehicle. But like every car they passed, the driver had abandoned the vehicle.

They had less than two miles to go before they reached home, and as they crawled along the road, he was eager to get there and relax. At least for a minute.

"Let's give you a pill now," Melissa said as she opened the bag and retrieved a bottle.

"What kind is it?" Jason asked her.

"Amoxicillin. The same stuff the doctor gave you when you had that infection. Remember?"

"Yeah."

"Do you have water still?"

Jason nodded. "Uh-huh."

Melissa shook out a pill and handed it to Jason, who swallowed it with a sip of water.

Glad that he was getting started on antibiotics, Alex felt a small smile start to lift the corners of his lips, but when the truck started to sputter, he pressed his lips together in frustration as he looked at the fuel gauge. It was on E.

"Great," he muttered.

"What's wrong?" Melissa asked.

"Looks like we're about to run out of fuel."

"We passed a gas station a little ways back," Jason said.

Giving him a half smile, Alex said, "I don't think that one sells diesel."

Jason sat back with a frown. "Oh."

It was at that moment that the tank ran dry, and as the engine cut off, Alex steered the truck to the curb. Not that it mattered. It wasn't like they had to get out of the way of traffic. It was more a habit than anything else.

"What about siphoning fuel from one of these cars?" Melissa said. "I mean, if they use diesel."

"That would be a great idea if we had a hose and a container to put the fuel in."

"We don't have that much farther to go," Melissa said with

a look of uncertainty. "We could walk home and come back later for the truck."

Alex considered that, but knowing how critical having a working vehicle was, he didn't want to take a chance if he could help it. "Maybe we can find something in one of these cars to siphon with." One side of his mouth quirked up. "It's worth a try at least."

With the truck stopped, all three got out.

"Hey," Jason said, pointing farther down the road. "That truck has landscaper tools in it. Maybe they have a hose we can use."

Hope climbing, Alex gave Jason a hearty slap on the back. "Great idea, son."

Jason beamed.

The trio trooped toward the landscaper's truck with Jason not limping too badly. A tipped-up wheelbarrow was tied to the wooden-slat sides of the truck bed. In addition, the truck bed held a lawn mower and several other tools. Including a hose.

Grinning, Alex climbed into the bed of the truck and picked up the hose. He held it out to Jason, who took it and set it on the pavement. Looking around to see what else could be useful, when Alex saw a five-gallon gas can strapped to the side of the wood slats, he nearly shouted for joy. Instead, he liberated it and handed it to Jason, then jumped to the pavement.

"Feels like there's gas in there," Jason said.

"Yeah, but it's gas, not diesel. Probably for the lawn mower. We'll have to dump it so we can use the can."

"Dump it on the ground?" Melissa asked.

"No. I'll put it in the truck's tank. Seems like a waste since the truck won't run, but we have no use for it."

After emptying the gas can, which was about half full, into the tank of the landscaper truck, Alex grabbed his tactical knife from the sheath at his back, then cut off a short length of hose. "Now to find a vehicle that runs on diesel."

CHAPTER 35

Melissa

"How can we tell if it's a diesel vehicle?" Jason asked.

Melissa was wondering the same thing.

"Open the fuel door," Alex said. "Sometimes it will say something about diesel. Also, if the fuel cap is green, it's diesel."

With that information, Melissa strode to the nearest vehicle, a midsize car. Pretty sure it wasn't diesel, she decided to check it anyway. She opened the fuel door. Nope. It didn't have either of the characteristics Alex had mentioned.

The snow that had been floating down before was now coming down thicker. It seemed like it was starting to stick to the road now too. That meant the road was cold enough for it to not immediately melt off. Which, as she hurried to the next vehicle, made her think about her home and how they were going to heat it. They had a wood burning fireplace in their family room and they had a small amount of firewood left from the winter, but if that was going to be their only source of heat, how long would it last?

She pictured their family room and knew all five of them would need to sleep in there. That would be the best way to stay warm.

After checking two more cars and not finding diesel, she began to think the better play was to just go ahead and walk home. It wasn't too far, and she thought Jason was doing well enough that he could make it.

"Found one!" Jason called out a moment later.

Relief flowed through Melissa's chest. She trotted over to the truck Jason stood beside. Alex reached it a moment later, the short length of hose and the gas can in his hands. "Good work," he said to Jason.

After removing the fuel cap, Alex threaded the hose into the tank, then he lifted the other end to his lips. "Here goes nothing." After grimacing, he put his lips on the hose and sucked. A moment later he began coughing and spitting. Even so, he shoved the hose, which had fluid flowing out of it, into the gas can.

"Let me," Melissa said, holding the hose in place while Alex worked to get the fuel out of his mouth.

Alex rinsed his mouth out with water from a water bottle that Jason handed him from his backpack.

"That was nasty," Alex said, his lips twisting in disgust.

Wondering how often they would have to siphon fuel and

if she would have to do it, Melissa puckered her lips in solidarity.

"The can's almost full," Melissa said.

Alex pulled the hose out of the truck's fuel tank and the fuel stopped flowing into the gas can. Next, he screwed the lid onto the gas can, then he carried it to their truck with Melissa and Jason walking beside him. At the truck, he removed the cap and attached the nozzle before pouring the siphoned fuel into the tank. When he'd emptied the gas can, he screwed the lid back on and tossed it and the short length of hose into the bed of their truck, then the three of them got back into the truck.

Feeling how close they were to getting home, and hopeful that nothing else would stop them, once Alex got the truck started again and they began moving forward, Melissa let herself relax. Just a bit.

As they drove through the area that was so familiar, a smile lifted her lips. They were nearly home. The turnoff to their neighborhood was just ahead.

Alex eased into the right turn lane, but when he reached the corner, Melissa saw several cars parked end to end, blocking the entrance to their neighborhood, and four armed men standing guard.

"What the...?" Alex's words trailed off as he stopped the truck about thirty feet from the blockade.

Melissa's heart began to pound and her anxiety skyrocket. What was happening? They had to get home to Emily and Steven.

"Wait," Alex said as he squinted toward the men who were now staring at them. Two of the men were pointing rifles at the truck. "Isn't that Tom?"

Melissa studied the four men who were all bundled up against the cold, which made it a little harder to recognize them. "Yeah," she finally said when she recognized one of their neighbors. "It is." She turned to Alex. "Do you think there's been trouble in the neighborhood already? Is that why they're there?" Which only made her desire to get to her younger children all the more intense.

"I don't know. When Jason and I left yesterday evening, everything was quiet." He paused. "Maybe they're just taking precautions." He put the truck in neutral and engaged the emergency brake. "Only one way to find out."

"I'm going with you," Melissa said, growing more anxious than ever to get home.

Alex nodded, then shifted his eyes to Jason. "Stay here."

Jason nodded. "Okay."

Once Alex got out of the truck, Melissa did the same.

"Let me see your hands," one of the men yelled at them, his rifle trained on them, which made Melissa's heart race. She threw her hands up and saw that Alex had raised his as well. This whole thing felt super odd. This was her neighborhood. These were her neighbors. At least Tom was. She didn't recognize the others, but then their neighborhood had several dozen houses. She didn't know everyone. Not by a long shot.

"Tom," Alex called out. "It's Alex and Melissa Clark."

"Alex?" Tom said. Then he said something to the other

men, who lowered their weapons. "You can put your hands down," Tom said to Alex and Melissa.

Exhaling a sigh of overwhelming relief, Melissa let her arms fall to her sides. A few moments later they reached the men.

"What's going on?" Alex asked.

"After what happened last night," Tom began.

"Wait," Melissa said, her heart thudding dully in her chest. "What happened last night? We weren't home but two of our children were. We need to get home to check on them."

"Of course," Tom said. He swiveled to the men beside him. "Let 'em through." Then he turned back to Tom and Melissa. "There was a home invasion a few streets over. Killed everyone in the house."

Melissa gasped as a chill raced through her. "Whose house was it?"

"The Fletchers."

Melissa didn't know them but it didn't make it any less horrifying. "Do you know who did it?"

Frowning, Tom shook his head. "No. But the place had been ransacked. We're just..." he waved his hand toward the blockade, "we want to keep track of who comes and goes from the neighborhood."

"Good idea," Alex said. "I'd like to help."

"Sure. We're having a community meeting tonight at the elementary school. Six o'clock."

One of the men who was guarding the entrance got

behind the wheel of Toyota Prius. The other two men pushed the car until a hole had opened in the blockade.

"Drive on through," Tom said.

With nod, Alex said, "See you tonight."

Melissa walked briskly back to the truck with Alex by her side. "I'm worried about the kids."

"I'm sure they're fine, but yeah, I know what you mean."

They got back in the truck and Alex drove forward, passing the blockade. A few moments later they turned onto their street, which wasn't far from the entrance to the neighborhood, and then into their driveway. Melissa only waited long enough for the truck to come to a stop. With the engine still running, she jumped out of the truck and raced to the front door. Once there, she twisted the doorknob, but it was locked. That wasn't unexpected.

"Emily!" she called as she dug through her purse for her keys. "Steven!"

Finally, she found her keys. With hands shaking a bit, she inserted the key and turned the deadbolt. By the time she was turning the knob, Alex and Jason had joined her. She pushed the door inward and stepped into the entry. "Emily! Steven!"

A moment later she heard thundering footsteps from upstairs, and then the kids appeared and ran down the stairs.

"Mom!" Emily said, throwing herself into her mother's arms. Steven wasn't far behind.

Melissa pulled him into her arms as well. She savored the group hug, but after several moments, she released her children, a broad smile on her lips.

Emily stepped back and smiled at Alex. "You found her."

Alex beamed. "Yes."

Reaching for Emily's face, Melissa asked, "Are you okay?"

Emily's eyes shone like she was about to cry, but she nodded and smiled.

"Let's go sit down," Melissa said.

"I'm going to put the truck in the garage first," Alex said.

Melissa nodded. Alex went into the garage, slid the door open, then drove the truck inside. He killed the engine and closed the garage door, then he joined Melissa and the children in the family room.

Melissa settled onto the couch and Alex sat beside her. Jason stretched out on the loveseat, setting his foot on the armrest, which elevated his leg. Steven sat on the fireplace hearth and Emily sat on the recliner.

Melissa looked first at Steven then at Emily. "How was it last night?"

Emily glanced at Steven then met her mother's gaze. "It was scary. So dark, and with you guys not here..." She grimaced then shook her head. "I'm just glad you're home."

Melissa gave her a warm smile. "Me too."

"What happened to your leg?" Steven asked Jason, evidently just noticing his torn jeans and the dried blood.

"I got shot," Jason said. Melissa couldn't miss the note of pride in his voice, like he had street cred now.

Emily sat up straight while Steven shouted, "What?"

"Yeah," he said with a grin and a gleam in his eye, "we were walking, and this guy started shooting at Mom and

Dad, and I..." he visibly swallowed and shifted his eyes to Alex.

"Jason jumped in front of us," Alex said, his voice shaking slightly like he was trying to control his emotions.

"Are you okay?" Emily asked her older brother, her forehead deeply furrowed.

"Yeah," Jason said. "It's just a flesh wound."

"We need to find someone with medical knowledge to take a look at that," Melissa said. "But let's at least get it cleaned up."

"Good idea," Alex said.

Melissa poured some water into a bowl, got soap and a washcloth, then gently cleaned the wound. Once she was done, she covered the wound in fresh gauze.

"Thanks, Mom," Jason said with a smile.

Thankful he was all right, she smiled back, then sat next to Alex.

"Now that we're all home," Alex said as he put an arm around her, "we have a lot of work to do."

Melissa leaned into him, filled with gratitude that she was surrounded by her husband and children and that everyone was safe. But now that she was with them, her thoughts went to the rest of her family—her younger sister Heather and her family, who lived several hours south of them, and her older brother Ben and his family, who lived in Los Angeles. How were they doing? Their parents had passed away a few years earlier, so it was just the three of them. Alex, on the other hand, had a younger brother who was married, as well as both parents, all of whom lived in Southern Utah, not too far from each other.

As much as she wanted to know how all of them were faring, short of traveling to them, there was no way to find out. For now, she needed to focus on her husband and children and what they had to do to survive.

"What do we need to do?" Steven asked, leaning forward like he was eager to get started.

Melissa imagined she would feel the same way after sitting around and waiting for twenty-four hours. Glad he had a good attitude, she turned to Alex to see what he had in mind.

"First off," he began, "we need to take an inventory of our food. See what we need and what we can barter with. Second, although we have some water stored, it won't last as long as we think, so we need to set up some sort of rain catchment system to increase our supply. We also need to get a fire started in the fireplace to warm this place up."

"It was really cold last night," Steven said.

"I was thinking we should sleep in the family room," Melissa said.

Alex nodded. "I was thinking the same thing. That fireplace is our only source of heat, and with this storm it's going to stay cold for a while. So yeah, we'll be spending a lot of time in here."

"This evening there's a meeting," Melissa added. "At the elementary school. We'll go to that and see what everyone has to say."

The kids all nodded, and as Melissa looked at each one of

them, her heart nearly overflowed with love. The most important thing was that they were together. She knew the future would hold many challenges and that none of them would be easy, but as long as they had each other they would get by. Not only that, but they lived in a great neighborhood with amazing people. She was confident they would manage to pull together and help each other out. They had to. Because going it alone would only make things more difficult. There was great strength in numbers, and she intended to do whatever she could to make sure she and her family and their friends were very strong indeed.

———

Thank you for reading Chaos Begins. The next book, Chaos Rises, will be released October 19, 2021.

In the meantime, if you haven't already, make sure and check out my Pandemic series, a series I wrote before the current pandemic. The four-book series is complete. You can see the first book, Pandemic: The Beginning, on Amazon.

ABOUT THE AUTHOR

Christine has always loved to read, but enjoys writing suspenseful novels as well. She has her own eReader and is not embarrassed to admit that she is a book hoarder. One of Christine's favorite activities is to go camping with her family and read, read, read while enjoying the beauty of nature.

I love to hear from my readers. You can contact me in any of the following ways:
www.christinekersey.com
christine@christinekersey.com

Made in the USA
Columbia, SC
21 January 2022